The Retail Therapist

Prequel to Blue and Green Should Never Be Seen! (Or So Mother Says)

COLETTE KEBELL

SKITTISH
ENDEAVOURS

COLETTE KEBELL

THE RETAIL THERAPIST
A SKITTISH ENDEAVOURS BOOK:

Originally published in Great Britain by Skittish Endeavours 2015

First Edition

Skittish Endeavours Books are supplied and printed via Ingram Spark

Printed and bound via Ingram Spark www.ingramspark.com

Thanks to:-
Design © www.Lizziegardiner.co.uk; illustrations © Shutterstock.com.
Proof-reader and Copy Editor: Patrick Roberts

For more information on Colette Kebell see her website at
www.colettekebell.com
or
follow her on Twitter @ColetteKebell
and/or
https://www.facebook.com/pages/Colette-Kebell/882613368417

CONTENTS

CHAPTER 1

Window shopping! Don't you just hate that term? That was what I had to do, at least until the end of the month, which was three weeks away!

At that point I had just left my job as a legal secretary, started a career as a personal shopper and was spending my wages faster than I could earn them. The fact of the matter was that I had expensive tastes, and insufficient funds to fulfil my desire for fashion; so here I was with my little notebook, looking at a Ted Baker shop from the outside and taking notes. I've done that for ages; when I see something I like, I write it down and revisit it the following month, when my meagre salary comes in. Don't get me wrong – I'm not a big fan of high-end designers; I think someone can dress properly even on a low budget, and that's what I do unless I decide to splash out all my salary in one go, as had happened this month. Not that I needed a notebook, anyway: I have a "fashion memory". Let me explain. In full accordance with Darwin's *On the Origin of Species,* by some freak accident of my DNA I can remember perfectly every shop, every item I saw in that shop, what exact colour each item was, and I also have the capability of matching it with my existing (huge) wardrobe. I can even match items that I saw months ago; if I were working in a hardware store selling paint, I would be employee of the month, every month! For the rest, it's a lot of bargain hunting; my regular trips to TK Maxx, for example, gave me a beautiful pair of Nicole Farhi leather trousers, a Fenn Wright and Mason dress, an Edina Ronay raincoat and loads more besides. Even places like Primark can spring a nice surprise on you if you choose carefully and you have that gift of matching clothes that I probably inherited from my Italian mother.

Oh, sod it! I'm gonna put that Ted Baker on a credit card; I'll pay the balance off next month.

The phone rang just one millisecond before I entered the shop, I looked at the display and it was Ritchie. I pondered for a couple of seconds whether I could ignore the call, and then I relented.

"Hello, Ritchie!" I said.

"Where are you, GiGi? We're all waiting for you." Bummer – I'd forgotten. It was Lillian's birthday and we'd decided to meet in a restaurant near Covent Garden to celebrate. It was a Mexican, and apparently they had the best tequila and vodka Martinis in the neighbourhood.

"I'm just three minutes away, literally around the corner; I'll be there in a jiffy," I lied. Well, I didn't lie completely: Floral Street *was* just around the corner, but I avoided mentioning my little detour in Ted Baker.

"GiGi, I know that tone in your voice! Tell me the truth – where are you?"

"I am telling the truth … I'm in Floral Street… I …"

"Are you by any chance near the Ted Baker shop?" How in hell had he known that? Had he installed in my bag one of those tracking devices you see in Hollywood movies? Had he planted a bug on my phone? Was he telepathic?

"Don't lie to me," he continued; "I walked that very road half an hour ago."

"Well, ahhh ... yes, but I was just window shopping, I swear," I lied again.

"If I see you enter the restaurant with a single bag in your hand, it will be confiscated, I promise. Possibly even given to a charity shop."

"I'm on my way," I said, feeling guilty and almost sobbing. "I'll be there in a minute."

Ritchie is an old friend of mine and has been since my school days, and I'm currently living at his place. He's also my sponsor. I'm on the path to recovery from spending too much on clothes. He made me admit that I had a problem (the first step) and he's keeping a strict eye on my spending habits. In some respects, Ritchie put me in "retail rehab"; I'm allowed to spend only a third of my earnings on clothes. Of the remaining two-thirds, one goes into a separate account, which is in my name but he keeps the online password hidden, and the other goes to cover the bills, expenses, etc.

I kept walking until I reached the restaurant, and there they were. I could see Lillian and her new boyfriend Blake, Helena and Adam, and of course Ritchie. No boyfriend this time, thank goodness. On that point we are similar and quite often we hang out with the wrong type of guy.

"Hey! What are those bags you're carrying?" asked Ritchie inquisitively, looking at the two bulging carrier bags I had in my hands.

"Presents. Aren't we supposed to be celebrating a birthday today?" I winked at Lillian, who in the meantime stood up and kissed me on both cheeks. Hopefully Ritchie would bury the hatchet for once and let me enjoy the evening. You know, he can be overprotective on occasion.

"Oh GiGi, you shouldn't have," said Lillian, receiving the packages. Wait until you see what's inside and you'll take your words back, I thought. "May I open them now?"

"Sure, go ahead; knock yourself out."

She opened the first one and the table fell

silent. It was a Roberto Cavalli dress, in a brown-and-blue diamond design with a smattering of gold thrown in for good measure, and I was sure it would fit her perfectly. I had been on a secret mission to find something for myself, in one of the underground warehouses that deals with discounted fashion items and samples, when one of the employees, a friend, pulled me into a corner. That item had arrived the previous day; there were no choices of size or anything and he'd hidden it under the counter, waiting for me to come into the shop. He knew I'd appreciate it.

In my personal-shopping business you have to have the right connections; the ability to find good clothes before everybody else does is paramount. And as soon as I saw the piece, the second person on my mind was Lillian; and at a hundred and fifty pounds it was a real bargain. Yeah, I got a special price, but I'd spent millions in that place – or at least that's how it felt – and they could afford the discount.

"Oh, my God! GiGi, is this a joke? Tell me it's real!" Her eyes were going from the dress, to me, and back to the dress again. If she could, she would have tried it on the spot. The second present was a bag that I thought would work well with the dress. This was an anonymous one, but who really cared? It was excellently made and nobody would be looking at the label anyway.

"Yep. That's the real deal," I added, proud of my catch of the day.

Ritchie was giving me killer looks, so I tried to ignore him. Not an easy task.

"So what are you up to these days?" she asked, after I'd removed my coat and sat down next to her and Blake.

"Oh, the usual: trying to change the world; not completely, I mean – just trying to make it look better." They knew my story only too well; the work I'd done for my first (unofficial) client Marianne, and the second one, with "Lady Gaga", an eccentric old lady who I'd transformed completely – from Cat-Woman into the Belle of the Ball, an achievement that earned me almost twenty grand. But I had lost that again; I'd put down the deposit on a house that I'd planned to buy with my boyfriend – but we split and now he was my ex. At that point I was broke and virtually homeless; thank God Ritchie took me in as a lodger. The overspending on my credit cards was the natural result of that frustration. I needed to gratify myself in some way and, not knowing how to mourn my earlier relationship, I went on a shopping spree. More than once. Ritchie had nominated himself as my guardian angel.

"So, Blake," I asked suddenly, "have you found a job yet?"

"Indeed I have; it's with a small firm of architects in Maidenhead. I'm there as a trainee, but so far, so good. And you – have you found any more of those strange clients of yours?" he asked.

"As a matter of fact I have," I said, and then I told them about my latest assignment, Vanessa, who had won the lottery.

"You mean that lady in Oxfordshire who got over thirty-five million a few months back?" asked Ritchie, incredulous.

"That very one; and it was thirty-five million plus pennies."

"How did you manage to get in touch

with her?" enquired Blake. The table fell silent for a moment.

"Actually, I didn't. It was Marjorie who put me in touch with her," I tried to explain, but the questions kept coming.

"You mean Cat-Woman?" interjected Lillian.

"Hey guys, let her explain," said Ritchie, coming to my rescue. A shame; sometimes I love a bit of suspense.

"The newly made millionaire Vanessa moved to Berkshire and bought a whopping five-million-pound mansion in Ascot, splashed another unspecified amount in having it redecorated and furnished, bought a spanking new flashy car – only to find herself alone, with more bedrooms than she needed. She was in her mid-forties, divorced, and wise enough to steer clear of any of the pretenders who suddenly popped up out of nowhere once they got the news about her new-found fortune. So what would you do if you were suddenly a millionaire? Surely you can't just pop into the neighbouring mansion and ask if you can borrow a cup of sugar. Think about it;

you have to dress up, jump in your Bentley and drive at least a mile to your neighbour, just to face a closed gate. Ringing the bell is no use; they don't know you and most likely the butler would just point you in the direction of the nearest Waitrose."

"Oh, come on, Gigi: get a move on! We're all going to die of thirst, if not starvation, by the time you finish this story!" one of them said, but I carried on regardless. I was, as usual, a woman on a mission to make the world a better-dressed place. I knew my friends from old and they knew me; they could put up with my storytelling just a little bit longer – that's the polite thing to do, isn't it?

"Vanessa was a woman of culture; she spent evenings in her mansion reading books and was actually an amusing person to be with. But she didn't have a single chance to interact with her peers, and was now very far removed from her old friendships, so life was starting to get boring. She was getting desperate by the time I was given her number. There is only so much travelling around the world you can do before you realise that life, even with money, can be tedious. Vanessa was shy by nature and, therefore, she wasn't the person to stand out at a social event. Not that she received any invitations anyway.

"An opportunity had presented itself a few months previously, when she'd rented a box for Royal Ascot. She'd been on the verge of leaving the racecourse, after just the second race. She couldn't manage to go to the neighbouring box and present herself; how in hell are you supposed to do that? 'Hello, I'm Vanessa.' People can be nasty and just answer, 'Who cares?' and like anybody else she wouldn't have liked to be rejected.

"So Vanessa decided to leave early, but just near the escalator she stumbled upon Marjorie, who had just tripped on the floor, with all the contents of her bag rolling around on the floor. Vanessa, who was a good-natured person, helped her to collect up her belongings – but her attire would have made anybody suspicious! In her quest to gain attention she'd gone dressed in full Essex style, with platinum-blonde hair extensions, eyelashes as long as a Halloween witch's broom, fake orange tan – the whole shebang. Her skirts had grown shorter and shorter as the months had passed, in an attempt to get noticed; that happened, of course, but for all the wrong reasons. Despite all that, Marjorie saw through the entire masquerade and realised she had in front of her a very nice person, maybe one that needed some help; so, moved, she invited Vanessa for a drink. One thing led to another and soon enough Vanessa was crying like a baby about her frustration at having all that money and no friends whatsoever."

"I thought Blake was long-winded," said Lillian, "but today you're putting him to shame."

"Come on, GiGi – get to the point," urged Ritchie.

"Oh well, I see you don't appreciate the short version of the facts. Ah, the mobile-phone generation! Everything has to be a hundred and forty characters nowadays." I tried to look disappointed, but I was sure my face had a weird expression, as they all started mimicking me. I couldn't have cared less if they got bored; it was my story, after all.

"So the good Marjorie, fresh from getting the GiGi treatment, sent Vanessa in my direction for a makeover. Vanessa had a nice figure and plenty of cash to spend; during my initial assessment I asked her if she wanted something that looked good but not expensive or if she wanted the high-end stuff. The answer was always the same; everybody wants high-end garments. So I did a little experiment on her; I proposed a mix of the two without her even noticing. I showed her how to enhance her figure without being tatty and to look elegant without spending a fortune. It doesn't matter whether you've won the lottery; you don't have to go around wearing thousands of pounds' worth of clothes all the time – a few well-chosen items make all the difference. Especially if you knew a few of the tricks I've learned on my journey so far."

"So, are you now a millionaire as well, then?" asked Lillian.

"I wish! No, I'm not, but all this is giving

me confidence that there is a market out there, with people who are willing to spend money to look beautiful." I tried to pontificate, as if I was in front of Peter Jones attempting to convince him to invest in my little endeavour.

"We're still missing the finale," interjected Ritchie.

"Marjorie invited Vanessa to dinner with a few friends," I explained, "and of course Vanessa's witty personality came out. The fact that she was also looking the part boosted her confidence. Rumour has it that she may even have found a boyfriend – a nice one."

I was almost expecting a round of applause, but our plates arrived at that very moment and we all became busy getting spiced up with Mexican food. We did, however, enjoy our meal together and declared the birthday bash a huge success, partly due to the presents, but mostly because of the company and good food.

CHAPTER 2

So, how did I start being a personal shopper? Easy. I worked as a secretary first; to be precise, as a legal secretary. My first secretarial job was in a firm of surveyors; it was as boring as watching grass grow and paid peanuts as a salary. My monkey period was over, I thought soon enough, and I was on the hunt for a change. I found my second job in Farnborough, after weeks of scouring the internet and visiting one agency after another in the search for that elusive occupation. I had almost given up and decided to look at temping when the call arrived. The Office Seraphim's Agency (or something like that) had found my CV somewhere, on one of the millions of job websites where I had posted it, and wanted to put me forward for a new position for which they'd just received details. The post was apparently an opportunity that happens once in a lifetime – to become a legal secretary for a renowned firm established more than forty years ago, Lowe and Partners. No legal experience was required, though.

Hey, when a chance like that comes along you snatch it up, don't you? The agency didn't even want to have a preliminary interview. The chap on the phone was pleasant enough, and when I said I was a fast typist (which I was) there was no reason to mistrust my assertion. They organised a meeting with the senior partner for the following Monday, and there I went. I was thrown into the glamorous, desirable world of legal secretariat. Fortunately enough I had time for a trip to the outlet to buy some proper office clothes. You have to spend money to make money; don't they always say that on *Dragon's Den*? Surely, we would have to deal with high-end conveyances, large inheritances and divorces, and I wanted to look the part.

The interview was surprisingly brief. I went to their office on a Monday at lunchtime. The office was situated above a Chinese restaurant, with the entrance just on the left – a blue door with a metal plate, well worn, reading "Lowe and Partners". The wood was rotten at the bottom of the door and the paint was peeling off after years of rain and sun. I climbed the steps and introduced myself to Eliza, a South African lady as slim as a stick, with big, thick glasses, who was working as secretary and receptionist. She looked miserable, like a dog that had been beaten up and kept on a chain all day long, without even the hope of a walk or even being able to have a sniff around. Lowe interviewed me first, an old man in his seventies if he was a day, well dressed and with a strong German accent; and he was followed by his wife, who resembled a wicked witch. I didn't get exactly what the wife was doing in the firm, but at that time I was too shy to ask. For sure, she wasn't a solicitor and neither was she a secretary; I soon had the suspicion that perhaps she was just there to keep a close eye on her husband. Perhaps he was an old pig.

The interview didn't strike me as very professional: just a couple of questions about my previous job, whether I had any experience and whether I was a fast typist. Something didn't add up: no questions about my motivation, why I wanted that job, where I saw myself in five years' time ... you know – the regular bull that everybody asks in those situations. They didn't seem to be too fussy when it came to hiring. Seraphim's called me that very afternoon, informing me that I'd got the job and I could start the following week.

I broke the news to my partner that very evening; he couldn't have cared less.

"It's your decision," he kept repeating like a parrot; not a single word of encouragement or even the willingness to spend some time discussing the matter. After all, if I was going for a higher-paid job it was for us, our future, not only for my little passion for clothes.

I spent the first week without any hassle, learning about forms and on occasion answering the telephone. Lowe's wife, meanwhile, was flying around like a condor looking for carrion, always ready to grumble if someone spent an additional millisecond chatting about something that wasn't work-related. Most likely she was even setting a stop watch to gauge how much time the personnel spent in the toilet.

I went for lunch a couple of times with Eliza and finally, after some fishing, I found out what was wrong with that job. The old boy had already lost five secretaries that year and was able to drive everybody nuts. After a couple of months of mistreatment, the clever ones left for another job. Lowe and Partners was the name of the firm, but the first question popping into my mind was, *Where the bloody hell are the partners?* I could see only the old fellow and two junior solicitors, and partners they were not, I was sure of that. I could clearly see they had the exact same terror in their eyes as Eliza had.

"But ... didn't they tell you, at the agency, who you were going to work for?" she asked, surprised.

"Apparently not. They talked to me on the phone and they thought, 'Here's the solution to our problems.' " I laughed, but I didn't think it was actually a very funny situation.

"Every agency in town knows him; I'm surprised there are still some agencies that want to work with him. Whenever I've had to call them saying we needed a new secretary, most of the time they've hung up on me."

"So, why are you staying?" I asked curiously. Maybe there was still hope.

"My husband and I are saving to go to Australia. Paul has two sons working there already and if we transfer, we can have his other son move there from South Africa, on what's called a 'family ticket'."

"Don't you have to have a job, to get into Australia in the first place?"

She laughed out loud. "No, we're going there as pensioners. As long as we have enough funds for the first two years, before the pension kicks in, that's allowed. That's why I'm still working here; we're saving as much as we can."

I was stuffed. I still had thirty-four years to go before retirement.

I had to swallow the medicine the following week. Eliza was safe because mostly she was working as the receptionist, but I could see she was terrified, always trying to appear busy at the computer. For me, it was a different matter; I had to type all the letters that old Lowe had dictated, with headset on and nothing much to do other than type. The problem was that the old oaf was speaking quickly, with a German accent despite his forty-odd years spent in England and most of the time he was mangling the words. I could barely understand what in hell he was saying. The worst were the names, which he pronounced wrongly all the time. For those; I had to go and get out the old files to try to find the correct spelling, hoping that the previous secretary had done their job properly in writing it correctly. That was an endeavour not without risks. And then, at the end of the day it was "correction time". Every time there was a mistake, the old boy became a fury.

"VAT ZE HELL? ZHERE IZ A MISTAKE HERE! Vhy can you not type properly? Vhy all the idiotz come to vork for me?"

Usually the tirade lasted for about thirty minutes, and answering back was of no use.

Just mentioning that in that half an hour I could have corrected all the letters and been on my way home was of no use. His face often became red; then typically he started throwing files on the floor and pacing back and forth between his desk and the window.

As soon as he had finished, his wife would come out of her slumber-room, asking what had happened. And just when I'd become busy trying to correct the bloody letters, then she started, explaining to me: "We have to be precise, and those papers are going to be used in court, and if they are not correct it would be a major issue" – and blah-di-blah-di-blah.

I looked at Eliza and she shrugged, as if to say, nothing new on the western front.

My boyfriend was not sympathetic either; he kept repeating that life was hard and we should be glad that at least we had a job. Whenever I complained, he answered back that it didn't look good to have too many jobs on your CV.

The problem was that the more old man Lowe put me under pressure, the more mistakes I made. If he had just marked the errors I would have had them corrected in no time, but where was the fun in that? Eventually, one day, he caught me in a bad mood. When he called me into his office for the usual "corrections", I emptied my cup of tea on his desk and calmly and politely told him to f… off. Just to be sure, I repeated that concept to his beloved wife. When I left, Eliza was looking at me as if I were her personal hero.

CHAPTER 3

My mother kept nagging at me that I should have found my own place, as I was hijacking every possible space in their home with my clothes, shoes, bags and coats; and that's not counting all the things, the day-to-day stuff, that I had at Ritchie's apartment. There's a thin line between loving fashion and being a hoarder, believe me.

So, I started being a personal shopper by chance. In addition to being a secretary I had a job as a nanny, and the lady of the house needed some assistance. Needless to say, my suggestions were spot-on and made a huge impression among the upper crust in Berkshire, so, by word of mouth, I started receiving other "requests for assistance" – and there I was.

It's not as easy as you might think. I spent the day scavenging around shops, looking at clothes on the internet, keeping up to date with the latest trends; it was like being on a diet and working in a chocolate shop. Life is hard, but someone has to do it, I say.

Now, despite not knowing anything about information technology, and after days spent fighting with HTML code and mostly pleading, rather than asking, for help from friends, I also have a website.

I was home trying to work out a lead a former client had thrown at me when I heard the door slamming. I closed the laptop and went to see why Ritchie was home so early; it was eleven in the morning and that was highly unusual.

"The bastards!" he shouted as soon as I entered the lounge. "I can't believe that!"

"What's going on?" he was walking up and down from the sofa to the window and back, biting his nails as he usually did when he was nervous.

"They fired me," he continued, "or, as they say, they 'let me go'. Redundancy and all that rubbish."

"Hang on – sit down," I urged him. "Calm down for a second and tell me the whole story."

"There isn't much to tell. Do you

remember little Frank, the one who was made supervisor instead of me, just because he has a brown nose?"

"As a matter of fact I do. Isn't he the one who has no issues whatsoever with authority?" I added sarcastically.

"Cheap shot! I just don't like being told what to do; you know, I have ideas of my own."

"OK – so what about Frank?" I started wondering if he had punched him in the face or had thrown him down from the balcony in Selfridges. The two had always been like cat and dog.

"He called me into his office, made the speech that they were reducing the personnel and all the other crap. They also had my P45 already there. They could have had the decency to let me know a few days earlier. In this period finding a job is not easy."

I wasn't sure at that point whether he was more upset because he'd lost his job, which he hated anyway, or whether it was because Frank had been the one to fire him. Knowing him well, though, and if he'd got the supervisor job in the first place and had had to fire someone, he wouldn't have done it; Ritchie would have told his superiors what to do with their redundancy plan and would have lost his own job anyway.

"You'll find another place, Ritchie. You're good at what you do and you love fashion. Someone out there will recognise your talent." I tried to cheer him up, but it was a hopeless task. When he was in such a foul mood he just had to vent his frustration, before eventually coming to his senses.

"Oh my God – how am I going to pay the bills, if I don't find something soon?" I knew very well the guilt trip he was experiencing. He had just spent a fortune on a cashmere coat and now he was going to regret the purchase, biting his nails until they started hurting.

"I can give you a hand on that. Vanessa just paid me."

"GiGi, I can't let you do that. Come on."

"So, we both have to go back to our parents, tails between our legs, and beg them to let us have our little rooms back?" I snapped, "How's that as an option?" I knew that if I played the parent card I had a chance; it was also my place, that apartment, even if it was only on a temporary basis. "Think, Ritchie: I've just been paid, and you made me save all that money for a rainy day. Looks to me like today it's pouring, so why not?"

He mulled it over for a couple of minutes and then nodded; one less problem to take care of.

At that point my mobile rang.

"GiGi Personal Shopper – how can I assist you?" Ritchie looked at me, flabbergasted, most likely owing to the lack of imagination in my business name. But at that point people already knew it and also I was listed in the directory and on the web, so no point in changing it. I put my index finger on my lips, signalling him to keep quiet.

"Yes … of course, Natalie ... what do you mean exactly when you say 'a fashion emergency'?"

Ritchie at that point looked amused and I was glad, for once, that he had kept quiet instead of making one of his silly jokes.

"I see ... sounds urgent. Let me check my schedule ... yes, I think I could make this afternoon. I'll have to reschedule another appointment but hey, an emergency is an emergency." The woman gave me the address and contact details and we parted with the promise to meet a few hours later.

I hung up the phone and asked, "Do you want to come along?"

"Ummm ... no, I think I should start preparing my CV." He didn't look convinced and I know that starting to amend a CV the very same day you've been made redundant is a sure recipe for depression.

"Oh, come on. You need some fresh air and the CV can wait until tomorrow. And you might actually enjoy it."

"So, where is your emergency?" he asked. Fortunately, his curiosity took over.

"Windsor. A certain Allyson Taylor is being interviewed by a magazine in a couple of weeks' time and she recognises her wardrobe is not up to scratch."

"*The* Allyson Taylor? The one from the Berks Girls, the series on telly?" I didn't have a clue what he was talking about, but Richie knew his television programmes; I guessed she was probably a minor celebrity, considering she was going to be interviewed.

"Well, you can tag along and see for yourself. I might even be able to get you an autograph," I teased him.

"Ha, ha, very funny. Only thing is, I can't come. I have to get my CV updated and putting it off won't get me anywhere fast! The autograph would be greatly appreciated, though," he added with a wink. I had often wondered just how many different things Ritchie collected. I've seen that there is very little space at his place for me to occupy, owing to his "collections", but he's so damn secretive about them; they're never on display. One of these nights, when he's either out or fast asleep, I vowed I would investigate. No man, be they gay or straight, could seriously be that much of a hoarder, could he?

CHAPTER 4

Following Lowe and Partners I found another job as a legal secretary at Hutchinson and Rake. The first impression I got of the place was the sense of how cold it was. Sure, it was winter, but inside the office I felt almost as if I could see the condensation coming out of my mouth. I shrugged and thought that maybe I was getting a cold, or perhaps the office was inhabited by ghosts. I'd seen it in a film once or twice – that when a ghost passes nearby, you get a chill. That place must have been bloody haunted then; maybe in its early years it was a ghost assembly point for the afterlife.

Rebecca and Leonard were the partners and they were sympathetic, knowing I had spent all that time working for Lowe and Partners. Perhaps they had the same feeling you get when you go to the Battersea Dogs' Home and rescue a dog. If I had been able to stick it out at that old place for that long, it certainly showed tenacity and perhaps they saw potential in me; anyway, the fact is that I was hired on the spot.

I was to work with Penny (and no connection to Miss Moneypenny from the Bond films), who was also the Practice Manager, in a small room too cramped to have two chairs and two desks in it. Well, actually the workstations would fit in the room, but with all the folders dispersed around as well, the small size of the area meant that it was more like working inside a shipping container filled to the brim than being in an office.

In addition, Penny was not – how should I say? – the friendliest person on the planet. I entered the office that very first day and soon that cold, haunted feeling surrounded me. A quick inspection of the history of the building and a trip to the cupboard revealed the story behind that weird sensation. The boiler's thermostat was set to thirteen degrees. I reckon it was frozen solid in that state, perhaps since the last glaciation period; icicles were still there. I turned the dial up to twenty-two degrees (I thought it was a legal requirement for it to be above a certain temperature to work in; I remember reading something like that in a Solzhenitsyn book once).

It became evident that what I had thought was a simple oversight was in fact part of a carefully planned savings strategy. Rebecca insisted on working "a couple of degrees" below the "normal" temperature, because at the end of the year it would result in a massive saving. Not that my sneaky attempts to turn that bloody dial up a couple of degrees served any purpose: my colleague Penny was in that period of life where she felt hot (despite the fact that we were already working as though we were in an Inuit igloo) and she insisted on keeping the window wide open. Or a "tad" open, as she put it.

If you think about it, there were only two options: either you ask your colleague to come to work in a bikini (attire not compliant with the practice book), or you go to the office using a multilayer approach, like an onion. Despite my reluctance, I had to wear long johns under my trousers, thermal underwear, a jumper, body warmer and fingerless woollen gloves. The gloves took a while to get used to, though; at first it was as if I were permanently attempting to do the *Spock* thing with my fingers, or something like that. I'm sure you get the picture. I could have been in an advertisement as a Michelin Woman and I looked as if I was twenty pounds overweight at least.

I also soon realised that Penny had a second name: Grumpy. If she wasn't complaining about the weather – it was always too hot no matter what the season – she would find something to complain about in everything else. The way I was taking the messages, how I was paginating the letters and so forth. The fact that she'd worked for the firm for almost twenty years apparently made her think she was a de facto partner, and that gave her the right to make my life miserable. In that little room there was no escape from her constant bitching, and initially I thought I'd just escaped from the frying pan to land in the fire.

The months passed and I got to know the other secretaries as well. One was Emma, a woman in her late sixties, who always talked about her retirement plans. That was her pet subject, but despite all the talking, every morning she got up and took a bus and a train to get to work, no matter what the weather. Emma didn't actually need to work any longer, as her husband was well off, but I think she'd got stuck in that place. It sucked the life out of her and she reminded me of an animal in a zoo – so used to being caged up that, if once her jailer forgot to close the door, she wouldn't recognise the opportunity to be free again. She was working part-time at that point; she was just part of the furniture – a quiet and reassuring presence that reminded the rest of us what our future could be like. Then there was Martina. She was in her late thirties and perhaps too young to bear the signs, but the life that loomed ahead there was clear to me. In ten years I would become like her, then become a Grumpy colleague myself, only to end up like Emma. One thing I should mention, though, is that it wasn't all completely doom and gloom. We each had the benefit of annual leave and some made the most of that time. Exotic holidays were the order of the day, and the more exotic the better. As for luxury, they definitely went the whole hog when it came to their time away from the office. From skiing to all-inclusive beach holidays, those were the norm as far as most of my colleagues were concerned.

Having said that, the miseries in that place were never-ending and every day brought a new surprise, at least to me. The birthdays, for example: we did not celebrate birthdays like anybody else. Under Rebecca's diktat, celebration of all the birthdays was on the fifteenth of November, no matter if you were born in July. That ensured we didn't waste too many office hours on frivolities such as preparing or eating cakes but, most importantly, we saved money on gifts. Christmas? We did the secret Santa, as in every other office around the country, but that was also celebrated on November the fifteenth, and therefore we were allowed to give only one present, usually below the ten pounds mark, also set by Rebecca. Rebecca's passion for saving money was not limited to the above; every occasion could be good for saving, if you have the patience, or in her case the gift, of looking. We used the Post-it notes on both sides, even if the glue was on one side only. The technique was simple and concise. You could write a message on the paper, and when it became obsolete you would cross it out it with a pen and design a big arrow pointing to the right, suggesting you turn over the paper in order to find the newly written message. Then matters got even worse; instead of using Post-It notes, we even started having to use up the paper from junk faxes that we'd received.

Rebecca was also charging customers for secretarial hours. If we had to witness a will; that was ten pounds; if we had to type long letters, we would have to mark the time so she could charge it out. In science-fiction books you come across devices that allow you to alter time in some fashion; Rebecca would have loved having such a device so as to squeeze additional hours into your working day.

Despite this military precision in managing savings, the same attention was not applied to other matters, such as the typing queue. We had two solicitors and a trainee, and usually the rule was to pile up the case files and tapes and to type them according to their arrival time in the pile – first in, first out. The only exception was for emergencies; in such cases a solicitor could jump the queue.

The fact was, though, that everything in that place was urgent, and every day there was a constant switching of priorities. The solicitors would dance around the typing queue on a regular basis, usually three or four times a day – except when Rebecca had a real emergency, and then that would be a "priority one" no matter what. Unless, of course, Leonard was in a bad mood; then he would complain to Rebecca and take priority for himself.

Leonard hated clients. Any occasion was good for escaping the office and doing some court work, or anything at all that didn't include client meetings. I hadn't realised, at the beginning, the reason behind his grumpiness, but then a pattern started to emerge. Every time he had a meeting with a client, then his mood would be foul; he would practically scream the place down, sometimes bellowing his orders. If you saw him at that particular time, his face would often be red and blotchy from the anger he obviously felt. There had been times when he even physically shook from the rage he felt. He actually admitted, one day, that a world without clients would make his life easier. With that in mind, he started dumping on me every single task he could that involved talking to people. How he got married in the first place remains an unsolved mystery to this day. Any way you looked at it, he was a bit of a mess.

Taking sickness days was strictly forbidden, despite working in a freezer in winter, with an open window, and the only way to have them recognise sickness was to bring them a death certificate from the GP.

And then there was the biggest of all comedies: the end-of-year review. I entered the legal secretariat as a way of earning more money to fund my passion for clothes, but talking about pay rises was like talking about ropes in the house of one who'd been hanged.

Rebecca was full of resources; she could remember every single word you'd spoken during the year and, so it seemed, how you'd failed to be sufficiently cordial on one occasion. Despite praising your effort, your work was not good enough to earn you a bonus or a pay rise.

So, when one day I was given the opportunity of working as a freelance personal shopper, because an old family friend threw the job in my direction, I was glad to use all my accrued vacation to do it. When I realised I couldn't complete what I wanted in that twenty-day period, I simply didn't show up in the office. Up till now, they still think they fired me.

CHAPTER 5

The house was on the outskirts of Windsor and caused me to rethink my job. Blimey, if a minor celebrity could afford a detached like that, at least five bedrooms with an acre of land, then I was definitely in the wrong line of business.

I rang the bell and the lady of the manor came to open the door, accompanied by the mandatory golden retriever.

"You must be GiGi," she said, shaking my hand, and then looked quizzically at what I was carrying. Before she could ask I told her that I had been doing some research. Well, I hadn't actually, but love him or hate him, Ritchie had given me a mountain to read through; after her phone call it was obvious that, for whatever reason, he was a big fan. Had I missed the boat completely on this one, not watching much TV and all?

"I'm a big fan," I added (a little white lie

wasn't going to hurt anyone, was it?). I could see that Allyson Taylor hadn't decided yet if she wanted to go full Rihanna or mix in a bit of Daisy Duke. In any case, the result was unbelievable; in the wrong sense of the word.

I imagined you could have used stamps instead of clothes and covered your body more appropriately, or for that matter the straps worn by the character Leeloo in the film *The Fifth Element*; either would have covered her body with better effect. Allyson turned out to be very down to earth despite having been brought up amongst the Berkshire Elite, as it were. She led me to the kitchen – not the lounge as you might have expected – and offered me a glass of coconut water. I had never even heard of that previously, but it turned out to be quite delicious with only a mild coconut flavour, unlike the milk or flesh itself. I was then told of all the amazing qualities that drinking coconut water had to offer, and I have to say, she was a born saleswoman as she certainly had me convinced. She did explain, however, that her attire was due to having just completed her daily exercise routine, upon hearing which I heaved a huge sigh of relief. I may not have heard of the Berks Girls, but I had a vague recollection of catching a clip of *The Only Way is Essex* at some point, and I had envisaged that Allyson must have been in both, and picked up all the wrong habits from the latter! She told me of her up-and-coming interview and what it was she needed from me. She was so excited, as this was going to be a serious role for her, not some kind of reality TV thing. We talked for a while longer, about the role she was hoping to play, what time period it would be set in (which thankfully for me was the present, or almost, as I was hopeless when it came to period clothes, other than vintage 60s stuff, that is) and what she hoped to achieve following that. It was always good to plan ahead, but she seemed to be planning as far as her retirement already! She was a couple of years younger than me! Had I missed something during my upbringing? Why did she make so many plans? I wanted to ask her, but felt it would be rude at this point. She hadn't even decided whether to employ me or not yet, after all.

And so I was shown to her dressing room. I have to say, other than in films like *Overboard* – starring Goldie Hawn – I've never seen quite such a beautiful room, filled with the most gorgeous outfits. It wasn't until I looked a little closer that I saw her dilemma. All her outfits were either for keeping fit or for evening wear. She was obviously quite the party-goer, as at a guess there must have been hundreds of evening dresses. At last I was starting to get the picture of what she needed.

"I see," I said, after a long pause. "I think you need something conservative, yet flattering. Something that you might use at home, or for tea with friends. The 'non-special' occasion."

"You got it!" she exclaimed, as if she'd just won the lottery "I didn't explain myself well, but I was sure I couldn't go to an interview in an evening dress."

"… and you don't know where to start, because finding something that matches your personality takes time," I added.

"That's it, GiGi. They told me you were good. You clearly understand the dilemma here."

I asked her which colours she preferred and what type of style, and then we sat down at her computer so I could show her a few examples of what would suit her for her interview. She was enthralled, to the point of complete silence, the whole time during this process. Once I was done, she took one look at me and stated quite clearly, "You are most definitely hired."

The hard work began next – the negotiation – but as it turned out Allyson was indeed desperate to make a good impression and obviously didn't lack the funds, so my fee was agreed and so was the clothes budget.

"GiGi, may I ask you something?" she added as an afterthought, when we were almost ready to depart.

"Sure, fire away."

"Do you think one set of clothes would be enough? I mean, what if they come back because they've forgotten to ask me something? What if I have other people visiting?" She was clearly going back into planning mode; I could see her mind spinning.

"If you need more outfits, we can do it. Easy."

"Let's do that," she said, regaining her original enthusiasm. "Let's take the full week – I mean, if you're not busy."

I wasn't busy, but at the same time I was doing the part of Mr Wolf in *Pulp Fiction*: I was saving the day. "Let me check my diary." I opened the diary where I used to write down ideas and things that I saw in shops, mumbled a bit as if I had to call back Michelle Obama and cancel her appointment, and finally I announced, "Yes, we can do it. I'll have to shuffle some appointments around, but leave that to me."

She also gave me carte blanche to buy anything I thought suitable for her on her behalf and said she would reimburse me. The tricky bit came when I had to ask for a small advance, to cover expenses. I thought at first she was going to refuse, but after a few seconds she readily agreed to give me a thousand pounds to start off with. I was over the moon. I promised to return the following afternoon, which she preferred owing to her rigorous morning-exercise regime (and probably her late rising, with the amount of partying that she did – but who knows?), with my arms laden with outfits. She thanked me with a great big hug, which I hadn't expected at all, and off I went. I had work to do, or rather, *The game was afoot,* as Sherlock Holmes might have said.

It was still relatively early when I left and, as I was in Windsor, I headed straight to my favourite underground samples shop, which was not too far away. I was greeted with a big wave of the hand to follow my friend down the stairs, as the shop was quiet, but he was the only one there! It seemed that things had been a bit slow there recently. I hoped all that was about to change, not only for me but also for my favourite fashion haunt.

CHAPTER 6

Ritchie was like a tiger in a cage, walking up and down in the apartment without resting a moment; I could barely work. Another day passed with no phone calls, and Ritchie needed to get out of that house. He was driving me crazy. At first he started sending CVs and answering job ads as anybody else would; then the fear kicked in, knocking his confidence completely. He started adding his picture to the CV, so they could see what he looked like – "a more personal approach", he said; then he removed it when he still didn't get any response, only to add it again later. Then he tried different paper, using an expensive one; then a coloured one so that his CV could stand out in the pile. It was no use; every job received hundreds of replies and Ritchie, on paper, was just one of the many. The frustration mounted and he became bitchy, so something needed to be done.

"Hey, will you stop that? I can't concentrate," I said in a very irritated voice.

"Well, at least you're busy doing something. What are you doing, anyway?" he snapped back.

"Sorting out this Russian lady, who keeps dressing expensively but despite all her efforts still ends up looking like a Matryoshka doll."

"Can I have a look?" he asked, walking tentatively behind the computer screen I was staring at. "Oh my gosh – is that for real?" he said, looking at the picture of my newly acquired client, Ivana.

"Indeed; she's unbelievable, huh?"

"She's not bad if you remove the flowers, that heavy make-up and the stilts. Was she working in a Russian circus?" he added. "And look at that hair; she looks like Samantha Stephens from *Bewitched*."

"Now you're really being nasty," I said, but I already had that picture in my mind and started giggling.

"She could do with a sprinkle of Maria Grachvogel; she has the figure to carry the clothes and she wouldn't suffer by having some patterns to them. Just that alone would be a great improvement, without having a radical change. Well, it would be, but you know what I mean. Maybe with some Kamper jewellery, bold and square, and some Abcense shoes she wouldn't look that bad."

I was stunned. Where the frock was all that coming from? But the more I thought about it the more it made sense; what he was suggesting was right, although he had taken a completely different approach from mine. It would probably have fitted with her personality and Ritchie pulled off what I considered to be a miracle, considering he had never even spoken to the client. If he could do that from a picture, maybe he could do even better once he had some more details. An idea started forming in my mind.

"Ritchie, I was wondering … while you're searching for the perfect job, why don't you work with me on these assignments?"

"I don't know, GiGi; I have CVs to send out, as well as trawling the job sites and so on. And then I wouldn't know where to start," he added tentatively. As usual when nervous he started to bite his nails.

"It's just an idea," I continued, but my mind was spinning. "You could organise your day and spend a couple of hours searching for your job in the morning, instead of sitting at the computer all day long."

"Hmmm ..."

"And then you could help me out with some clients. I mean, I spend the day talking to them, driving, going to shops. I could use some help in keeping me sane and, mostly, in doing some research. I barely know some of the designers you mentioned, and if I wasn't paying attention to the fashion week I would've completely missed the point. I mean, I hardly have time to keep up with what's new."

"Hmmm ..."

"And you'd get paid. It's a real job: think about it," I pressed. I wasn't just trying to cheer him up; I honestly thought I could use his help, and my gut feeling was that he'd be great. It was a risk, but what had he to lose anyway? While waiting for that elusive job he could earn something, and do me a favour at the same time. Win–win.

Dinner was in Camberley, not too far from a couple of friends we shared, and that evening I forced him to get dressed, shave and come out of his room.

"And no, you can't bring your laptop; job agencies don't do night shifts!"

That made him laugh, for once, but since he'd lost his job he became obsessed about checking emails every ten minutes. He feared going to the loo, just in case someone might call for a position and he missed the call. "They move straight to the next one in line if you don't answer" – or at least that was his justification for not even going to pee. People need a break, once in a while, and I promised to myself I was going to give him one.

Knowing we were going out for dinner, my brother Dexter (or Dex for short) tagged along, hoping I would pay for dinner for him as well. He gave a brand-new meaning to the phrase "being between jobs", although I have to admit that on the rare occasions when he was in one he did work his socks off. He would grow up, eventually.

The venue was a fantastic Thai restaurant I'd found by chance in Camberley, not far from where we lived, and the atmosphere was exquisite. The interior resembled an old Tudor house, although the building itself was fairly new, and they had mixed British and Thai furniture in a very balanced way. Ritchie and I arrived last, as usual; they say women take ages to get ready. Ah!

Blake and Lillian were already waiting for us and so was Dex, accompanied by his girl of the moment.

"So what are you up to, Dex?" I asked, after I'd kissed him on both cheeks and he'd introduced me to his new girlfriend, a certain Jolie who, strangely enough, was far away in her looks from the bimbo style that had seemed to be his preference lately.

"More of the same; I'm between jobs" – that was no surprise – "but I keep myself busy now, as a football coach."

"Hopefully not for Chelsea?" asked Blake, who was passionate about his football. "Although granted,, you couldn't do any worse than the one in charge now."

"No, it's the local football team – the girls," explained Dex.

"What's that?" interjected Ritchie. "You weren't good enough to coach the boys?"

"Ha, ha, very funny. It has its responsibility, you know? Bonding the team, making them actually play together. They're teens, and there are days when I'm just grateful they simply show up for training."

"It's true," added Blake. "I was working with the Scouts in my spare time, and as soon as they reach their teenage years, somehow they disappear. We've all been there."

"We have the first match next Saturday," added Dex. "Do you want to tag along and show a bit of support?"

Football was not my cup of tea, but Dex needed some encouragement, so I agreed wholeheartedly to be there. And so did Blake and Lillian. "Ritchie, are you with us?" I asked my companion and best friend, who seemed to be miles away from what we were discussing.

"Aahhhh … yeah, sure! Count me in. Anybody want another round of beers?" he asked, standing up.

"Sure," answered Blake, "Let's see if the waitress is around …"

"Don't worry: I can order them directly at the bar; it's quicker," and without even waiting for an answer off he went. We continued talking about Dex's new endeavour when, by chance, I noticed Ritchie talking to a tall, muscular guy who had reached him from an adjoining table. They seemed friendly. Ritchie seemed completely engrossed, and was that a twinkle I saw in his eye? He was positively beaming when he returned to the table. One look was all it had taken. I could see very clearly that Ritchie, if only in his own head at that point, was in love. How could that be? He'd only talked to Mr Muscles for a few minutes, but I'd seen him tuck a piece of paper into his wallet, which could mean only one thing. His mood altered dramatically from that point on and, without meaning to, I saw all the surreptitious looks that were passing between the two of them. Dexter, on the other hand, was engrossed in talking about his teen football team. They seemed to have found at least something that kept them both occupied. Lillian burst out laughing and all heads turned in her direction. She, it seemed, had also spotted the looks passing between Ritchie and this new potential love interest of his.

"Ritchie has found a boyfriend: na na nan na na …" she started chanting, as if she were a six-year-old kid. She was giving the evil eye to Ritchie and just wouldn't stop laughing and chanting; she was trying to speak, but each time she started it came out sounding as if she was being strangled and the laughter just continued. Ritchie looked none too pleased, by the way. "What in hell are you laughing at, Lillian?" he said, quite upset and guilty, like a boy caught with the fingers in the Nutella jar. The boys interrupted their football talking and suddenly turned towards the two, as if they'd just missed a goal. Which they had, in a way.

"What's going on here?" asked Blake,

looking at his companion and then at Ritchie, missing the point.

"Nothing, dear," I interjected. "We're just having a bit of fun. Go back to your football."

Oh dear, Ritchie seems to be still taking this too personally, I thought. Lillian, having decided she was behaving in poor taste, was seriously trying to control herself, but with little effect. She eventually got up from the table and went to the ladies' room, presumably to regain some kind of composure.

"So, who's the Hulk?" I asked, trying not to giggle myself.

"It's just an old friend."

"No, he's not!" I pressed him.

"OK, he's not. We go to the same church."

"Ha, ha, ha!" I was glad he was starting to cheer up. "Sure. But you're too busy for a date. I mean, you have all those CVs you've got to send out, as well as keep minding the phone. You know …"

"I thought you'd just hired me as a fashion consultant researcher." He smirked at me.

"Indeed I have. I can give you a discount if you need my help in choosing your outfit."

"No thanks."

"I'm the best."

"I know you are, but no thanks."

"You forgot the beers, mate," interjected Dex, between a "Spurs" and an "Arsenal", leading me to think he wasn't really paying attention to what had just happened.

Ritchie got up again and went back to the bar. I could see he gave a quick glance at the Hulk's table.

CHAPTER 7

That was the way to work: Ritchie doing the research and phone calls, while I was hitting the road. The deadline for Allyson Taylor was close and the journalist would be there in just a few days. The clock was ticking.

I came home with bags of clothes and then we started sorting the best in Ritchie's bedroom; if we didn't consider something to be a perfect fit, we would have returned it to the shops.

"What do you make of this?" I asked, showing him a pair of pin-striped trousers and a jacket.

"Put that aside; that's perfect. Oh my gosh – I can't believe I'm doing this for Allyson Taylor," he said, full of emotion, "In that slave factory where I used to work we didn't have any celebrities."

"Well, now we have, and if we play our cards right, there might be more." It wasn't a false promise, word of mouth works wonders in my line of business and already I had landed work with some high-up people.

Eventually we finished the sorting and both of us felt we'd done an outstanding job. Ritchie went to the kitchen and opened a couple of beers that we drank there, sitting on the floor in his bedroom, admiring the result of our hard work.

"Do you want to tag along this time?" I asked him, while I was mentally rethinking about what went with what.

"I'll pass on this one. What happens if she doesn't like it? I'm going to take the blame."

"Don't be silly; she'll love it." I tried to encourage him, but I could see that being without a "proper" job had knocked his confidence out.

"Hmmm ..."

"OK, don't worry. Let's pack the things up and make a move."

We worked like a team, each knowing exactly what the other would think, like or dislike and I was happy Ritchie was part of this endeavour. If only it lasted; my job is a solitary one, even if I do happen to work with a lot of people. Having someone to share ideas regularly with made me realise that, if I wanted to go somewhere and fully enjoy what I was doing, I had to be with someone else – Ritchie, for example.

I took the car and drove to Ascot the same day; the boot was full to the brim with clothes, shoes and accessories and I had to make a person happy. The thousand pounds Allyson gave me were long gone and I invested my own to buy the necessary, but so be it, I thought. It's like being Father Christmas sometimes, and I thrive on joy when I realise I've made someone happy, even just for a moment. When people speak about job satisfaction, I get it; I know exactly what they mean.

Allyson Taylor was waiting impatiently by the window, while I parked my reindeer in her driveway. Max, the retriever, was jumping around my car as if an old friend, long lost, had finally arrived home, and Allyson helped me to bring the goods inside.

"No peeking!" I warned her.

The most difficult thing, other than not

getting the job done, is presenting the results. A woman is used to her own style, even if it is a horrible one, and accepting changes is the hardest thing we have to endure – I call it "the path to recovery". Allyson was no different, and when she saw what I'd bought for her, she was worried. I could read the shock in her face, at the idea of having to wear something she'd never worn before. People can panic in such situations; they can reject the whole job altogether. Just the idea that a stranger might know what suits you better is repellent. "How can this woman know my likes and dislikes? Should I trust her?"

There's nothing wrong in that; it's in our nature, but I'd picked up a few tricks on the way that allowed me to bypass that tense moment.

"Why don't you try something on?"

Allyson obliged accordingly. She tried on outfit after outfit, though the first was one of my experiments. Her first outfit to try on was one that I'd picked up in one of the underground shops and it had been made by a minor designer, one that most people would never have heard of. She loved it to bits and this just encouraged her to continue trying on the pieces I had brought her. There were a few little gems amongst the clothes, however, that I'd gone over my usual spending limit to pick up. What Allyson didn't know, though, was that the most gorgeous one, the one she'd adored from the moment she set eyes on it, was a House of Fraser Linea dress. It was a beautiful bright apple-green in linen, with a white flower-pattern design and cream/off-white beading detail around the neckline. There was also a Marks and Spencer black-and-white number which, despite having a flowing skirt, suited her down to the ground. With some expensive accessories I'd bought for her, it was perfect.

It took time, but eventually she saw in herself what I saw in her. It wasn't just looking good for the right occasion that mattered; you have to look the part no matter what, to ensure you can go into the most unexpected places and still find yourself stylish and comfortable.

We spent the evening talking about what

I saw in her, what triggered the style that I had proposed and how I saw it could evolve. For a woman who planned everything, that was gold. Some lateral thinking, coming from the outside, allows you to evaluate who you are from a different perspective.

"GiGi, you have been extremely helpful, and I shall be forever grateful. Natalie was right: you did wonders."

It was time to go, so Allyson got up and fetched her cheque book. I opened my folder and lined up all the receipts for the clothes I'd bought, but she just waved her hands, saying, "Nonsense. Just tell me the full figure."

"Allyson, in that case I shall keep the receipts. If there's anything you want to change, or if you have second thoughts, just let me know and I can return some of the items. It's all part of the service ..." She interrupted me by waving the pen she had in her right hand, a beautiful Montegrappa fountain pen in blue and silver, and then added "Just tell me the total."

"Well, that would be twenty-one

thousand and three hundred pounds."

She was ready to write the cheque, when a sudden thought came into my mind: "Allyson, may I ask you a favour?"

"Of course you can," she said, looking directly into my eyes, as if at that point I could ask her anything I wanted; even the moon.

I explained what I had in mind and she had no objection whatsoever. It was a relief. Sometimes life is made up of small details.

We departed as two old friends, and in some respects we were. There isn't much as intimate as working together and the bond that we'd created between us was way beyond anything else that might happen in a working relationship. But that was exactly what made my work so special, despite my mother saying it wasn't a "real" job. I thought about it more as a way of *making friends*. I would have done it for nothing (only joking on that point – I'd never work for nothing).

When I arrived home I was exhausted, and Ritchie was already in bed. I went into my room but I couldn't sleep, so I tried to vegetate by watching telly, in the hope that sleepiness would arrive soon. It would soon be the weekend and I had a football match to attend.

When I got up Ritchie was still asleep, so I decided to fix some breakfast. I shouldn't have done so; he was the one usually taking care of food, and to be honest I wasn't good at it. I could mess up beans on toast with my culinary skills, but sometimes it's the gesture that counts, isn't it?

"Hello, sleepyhead," I said when finally Ritchie popped out of his room. His hair was all messed up as if he was a scarecrow and he was walking like a zombie who had lost his way to the shopping centre. "Did you have a heavy night?"

"Oh, nothing like that. Do you remember Johnny, the guy I met in the Thai restaurant?"

"You mean the hunk? Sure I do; do I have to prepare breakfast for three?" I teased him.

"Ha, ha, very funny. No, he's not here. We went out for a drink yesterday, we chatted a bit and the last thing I remember were the second bottle of wine and the shots. Then everything else is blurred."

"So he didn't take advantage of you. What a gentleman – and an officer. Or was it the other way round?"

"Gee, we have a comedian in the house," he said, starting to wake up. Most likely it was the smell of bacon that was reviving him "How did it go with Allyson Taylor?"

I opened my bag and pushed an envelope onto the table in his direction. "That's your share of the loot," I said, and then went back to fill the kettle. I hadn't slept much the previous night and I needed a very strong coffee. So did Ritchie, by the look of him.

He opened the envelope and looked at the cheque for a moment, turning it upside down as if he were analysing its consistency. "There's an error; it's in my name."

"I know it's in your name; that's your share of the pie," I said. I was by the kitchen door, waiting for the kettle to boil and at the same time enjoying the reaction on his face, which went from dazed, to astonishment, and then to concern.

"GiGi, that is ten thousand, one hundred and fifty pounds!"

"I know what's in there. I was present when Allyson signed it. Hey, I've had an idea; maybe you could frame it, instead of cashing it? You got her autograph, after all," I teased him.

"But ... this is what I was earning in more than five months of my previous job. GiGi; are you sure? It's definitely too much." Now the guilt and the embarrassment were taking place. He'd done a great job and I had decided to split the fee in half; I was trying to bribe him and maybe convince him to keep working with me.

"No errors there and no buts. There will be rainy days as well, so just enjoy your well-deserved salary."

"OH MY GOSH, OH MY GOSH! Are you saying all this money is for me? For real?"

"Yeah, relax," I said. "I was thinking that if you're up for it, we could keep working together, fifty-fifty. What do you think?" He jumped out of his chair and came to hug me. I was the happier of the two, even if I didn't dare show it.

"What do I think? I think I love you, GiGi! I think I'm over the moon and I don't give a damn about going back to working in a shop like I did before. I have a new vocation."

"So we have a deal. Fancy coming to my brother's football match?" I asked, to lighten the atmosphere before we both started crying like a pair of babies in a nursery.

"Yeah, let's do that," he said, as he finally let me go from one of the most emotional hugs in history. "Hey? Do I smell burnt?"

Oh, shit! The eggs or the bacon? Probably both.

CHAPTER 8

"First match today then, Bro?"

It was a rainy, miserable day and the football pitch looked like a swimming pool, or maybe the match sponsor was a mud spa and they'd let the marketing manager go a bit wild.

The team, the Bray Saints, looked depressed and beaten-up even before the start of the match. They came to the game each one with their own different outfit, and despite the small crowd cheering them on they were barely talking to each other, or even showing any enthusiasm about being there.

"Indeed. It's a mess. They're lazy in training and we had a friendly match last week. A bloodbath: we lost six–zero: more like a bloody tennis score."

Brother was also in a bad mood. Football was his life and his passion, and losing was definitely not an option. He was clever and engaging, but somehow this new team was eluding him. They did what they were told, but they were also lacking in initiative.

"Who's the captain?" I asked.

"The tall brunette by the bench, the one carrying the balls; her name's Nala." He pointed in the general direction of the stands; Nala was dragging her feet, probably counting the blades of grass under her feet and moving at a glacial pace. It didn't sound promising.

Dex assembled the team around him and made his speech, quoting the most famous coaches of the past, the pride of being part of the Bray Saints, this being the first step of a long journey and, no matter what, it was giving their best on each occasion that would define them as individuals. Personally, I would have added a sprinkle of Churchill, but that was just me.

From the minute the match started it became evident that this was no ordinary football match. It was the re-enactment of Agincourt, where the poor Bray Saints played the part of the French. Despite every possible effort at playing, the poor team were overwhelmed; not only were their adversaries faster and better organised, but by the beginning of the second half they even looked taller and bigger.

The puddle of rain became bigger and bigger, so much so that the referee suspended the match during the second half, when it appeared evident it was a game somewhere between water polo and wrestling in the mud.

That was the good news, because the bad news was that the Bray Saints were losing seven to one. After an hour of shouting, suggesting tactics and encouragement Dex was drained; so he rested on the bench, head in his hands, without even the energy to complain.

I needed to do something, even if at that point I didn't know exactly what; after all, Bray was my home village.

"Do you mind if I go into the changing room?" I asked Dex, who looked like an advertisement for an anti-depressant before the cure.

"Knock yourself out. They are prepared and potentially a better team, but somehow they don't work together."

Slowly, I followed the girls into the changing room and the atmosphere was indeed grim. Three or four were sitting on a bench, suddenly very interested in their shoelaces. Two brunettes in the corner were bickering about their respective mistakes and blaming each other for what they had or had not done during the game. Nala apparently couldn't have cared less.

Football was not my forte and even if I grew up with a brother who could barely talk about anything else, my knowledge was minimal.

I left them licking their wounds and went out again onto the field for some fresh air. A word kept coming into my mind: "confidence". Yes, that was the point; they were lacking in confidence. They could play all right, but they definitely didn't believe they could win – that was clear. I was wondering if they didn't have trust in each other, but I soon discarded that hypothesis: if that was the case they would not have cared at all and ignored each other, which hadn't happened. Simply put, they needed a leader.

I was still pondering the matter when the girls finally came out of the changing room. I looked at Nala and her baggy, gothic attire and an idea started to form in my mind.

After every match my brother used to take the girls to the nearby park for a pep talk and for a picnic. In fact we had the car full of beverages and food, the latter prepared by my mother, because nothing was less appealing to me than spending time trying to put together some concoction that, inevitably, would be inedible and end up in the bin.

When we arrived at the park we soon realised that nobody really wanted to speak about the match, not even Dex (which was a first for him), and people just started minding their own business. Some of the girls sat together and talked about boys and school; I sat near Nala.

"How long have you been a Goth?" I asked.

"Oh, you mean this?" she answered, looking at her clothes as if it was the first time she'd seen them. "I don't know: maybe a year or so."

"Strong it is, the dark side of the force," I said trying to make my best impression of Yoda, which resulted in a quizzical look. That hadn't gone down well, so I ditched the Star Wars approach

"Ehm ... I mean: what is it that attracts you about those outfits?"

She pondered the answer for what seemed an eternity and then came out with, "I don't know."

Damn! I kept quiet.

And then she added "I guess I'm trying to be different."

"Different from what?"

She shrugged and then added, "I don't know."

This conversation was going to be a difficult one.

"I suppose I want to be different from everybody else," she eventually added.

I wanted to steer our talk onto a lighter subject, but she pressed on. "I don't think I like what I'm doing, at school and stuff; it's all so boring."

"We've all been there, trying to figure out

what we would like to do in our lives, who we would like to be and where we would like to go."

"And?" she asked with sudden attention.

"And what?"

"Did you figure it out?"

That got me thinking. About my job as a secretary, the difficulties I'd had to endure at school, and what I was trying to do as a fashion consultant – with the satisfaction followed by the grief when things were not going as expected. "I suppose I'm still working on it," I said, "But I have an idea of where I'm going."

"So what do you do?"

I explained what my job was and it sounded more glamorous than it was in reality.

"Wow. I haven't figured out what I'd like to do yet; I only know I don't want to end up like my parents."

"What do you mean by that?"

"I don't know." That seemed to be her favourite phrase "I suppose they're boring. They always do the same things: they go to work, they come home and complain about it and then they get stuck in front of the television for the whole evening. And the following day it's exactly the same. They aren't going anywhere in their lives and they seem to accept it; they've sort of given up."

How could I explain that that was more common than she thought? I wasn't much different from her parents and was still trying to find my own way in the world. I might well end up in twenty years' time with my dreams broken, returning to secretarial work. I too had idolised my parents when I was a kid, only to find out later, when I was Nala's age, that they were just ordinary people. There's nothing wrong in being "ordinary"; going to work, paying the bills, raising a family and ensuring the kids don't get lost is a hell of a job. It's less glamorous than some others, but nonetheless something to admire. I would have signed on the dotted line on the spot, if someone had assured me I could have done that job as well with my own kids as my parents had done with me and Dex.

"But you like football," I said, passing

some "polpettes" that my mother had prepared. Those were definitely a winner; she had obtained the recipe from an Italian friend – they were a sort of pattie made with minced beef, parmesan, potatoes, breadcrumbs and seasoning and then fried. Simple food but, hell, I could have scoffed the lot. She took a bite and showed her approval with a nod of her head.

"That, yes."

"It's a start; in some respects it's a better choice than mine of being a fashion consultant – I mean, less expensive. "

"I love the way you dress, it looks always … appropriate."

"Maybe we should go shopping together sometime." She looked at me enquiringly, so I added, "Don't worry, I won't charge you."

"GiGi, do you have a boyfriend?"

That was a sore point. I'd had a few, some nice, some not. "That's another thing I'm working on."

"Me too," she added, "me too."

CHAPTER 9

I had known Ritchie for quite some time and, like me, I guess he was a magnet for attracting the wrong kind of people. Or maybe it was our own fault, always falling for the wrong guy. Anyway, with Johnny "the Hulk" he had struck gold. The man was caring, affectionate, and the two together laughed as if there were comedians in the house. I knew I would have to find my own place soon, but that wasn't a worry. By that time business had picked up and I could afford to move out.

When I say it had picked up, I suppose that's not quite true. We had work, but we also had quiet times; however, as I'd agreed to employ Ritchie, I felt I had the obligation of paying him a full salary even during the idle times.

That evening I went for dinner with the new couple and they even organised a blind date for me. Gosh, if it was anything like the previous one it would be a disaster. First they tried to pair me up with a writer. I was curious enough – I mean, if you write you're supposed to have something to say, and that would have been a good start, I thought. In fact he'd had plenty to say – about his ex-girlfriend: how they'd met, what they'd done during the five years they'd spent together, how she was unappreciative, and how she had cheated on him. After an hour or so spent trying to concentrate on my food, I started to sympathise with the ex! Blimey, I was already thinking about someone else – anyone, after just one dinner! I hadn't seen him again.

The second was an IT guy, a manager from a multinational in Berkshire. He was gorgeous and I'd been hoping that he had fantastic deep eyes. Unfortunately, I hadn't managed to see them once, as he was too busy texting someone in the office; he excused himself several times and after a few more minutes had to take an urgent phone call. (*Don't you just hate it when someone doesn't even consider your feelings enough to turn off their phone during a first date?*) So he left the table and went outside. I sipped wine for a while and then placed my food order. I'd had a busy day and was as hungry as a horse, without the nosebag, of course.

When he came back he said, "Sorry about that; it was an emergency. Good, you've ordered ..." The waiter approached us again and suddenly the phone rang again. Another emergency.

So I promptly ordered dessert.

When he came back and the phone rang again, I gave him my most understanding smile, muttered something about "Emergencies happen..." and then as soon as he went into the garden to take his call, I slipped out of the front door. For all I know, he might still be there answering emergency calls.

So when Ritchie proposed a double date, I was twitchy. No, I was panicking.

"Sure, no problem," I said. "I know all the effort you're putting into finding me a date."

"Are you complaining? I've found you some wonderful suitors. If only you weren't so picky …" he sighed.

Never fall for that; I could have picked a fight straight away, but where was the fun in that? Better to wait and see who the new Prince Charming was and then have my revenge.

We drove to the restaurant; the Hulk was already at the bar and if I hadn't been careful I could easily have called him that, instead of Johnny. I'd picked up that bad habit from my grandfather, who used to have a nickname for everybody, so in the family we used to refer to relatives and friends using their nicknames – until eventually one of us made a huge gaffe. There had been a family friend at one time who closely resembled Captain Pugwash (*and yes, I do mean the one from that old children's series*). I'd almost slipped up and called him that on numerous occasions but, thankfully, had stopped myself just in time.

My date was nowhere to be seen, so we decided to have a beer until Mr Last-Minute decided to show up.

"So you're in the army?" I asked Johnny. Poor Ritchie was lost in adoration and could only babble, and so I had to hold the conversation.

"Indeed – I'm in the Household Cavalry, but we don't use horses any more, before you ask."

"I was going to actually; so what do you use nowadays? No shining armour any more?"

"Ha, ha, ha – no we ditched that as well, a long time ago, at least as far as day to day wear is concerned. If you happen to have a date with one of my colleagues, you can expect them to arrive in a tank."

I looked at Ritchie, who was surprisingly quiet, and asked, "So who's my date? And most of all, where is he?"

"I was just trying to text him … hang on … here. Stuck in traffic; he'll join us in five or ten minutes. Sorry about that."

I was just hoping he was worth the wait. "What about finding a table, in the meantime?" proposed Johnny *"Bruce Banner"*, a suggestion we were all too happy to take.

"I love this Indian," Ritchie opened up. "I've been here a few times and I think it's one of the few that still haven't adapted to the British taste."

"I know what you mean," added Johnny. "I spent some time abroad when I was younger; went to Italy and so on. Totally different flavours."

I got distracted by a tall, handsome guy with long, dark hair by the entrance, busy looking at himself in the mirror. He was wearing a nice grey cardigan, unfortunately paired with rust-coloured jeans that didn't quite cover his ankles, no socks and a pair of designer shoes in electric blue. The shoes themselves were stunning, but the whole ensemble was just plain awful.

"Hey, have a peek at the Snow White 'King' down there. I could swear he just said 'Mirror, Mirror on the wall…'," I said.

Ritchie and Johnny looked at each other and started laughing, "That, my dear, is your date."

Prince Charming spotted Ritchie and waved. I was doomed.

"Well, well, here is our dear Hugo. How are you, mate?"

"I'm grand; thank you for asking."

They introduced me to the guy and he

was damn attractive. Ritchie is good at picking handsome guys but sometimes he tended to overlook personalities, at least he does when he's trying to organise me a date – which was every other week. No point in telling him I'm perfectly capable of finding my own. He's like a worried mother sometimes, concerned I will never marry or find the right man.

The good Hugo was apparently also working for a large IT company, near Bracknell. How he came to know Ritchie was a mystery I wasn't willing to solve, not that night; I was just hoping Hugo wasn't gay. Well, that had happened once, on one of the blind dates Ritchie had arranged.

The man was gulping tequila as if we were in a cowboy movie and then, when we were ready to order, he switched to whisky.

He ordered a Braes of Bladnoch and the poor waiter looked at him as if he'd come from Orion.

"I'm afraid, sir, we don't have that brand," said the poor chap.

"What about a Fetterthouch Glenghover?"

Zip!

Hugo started questioning our taste in restaurant matters; I could read the disappointment on his face.

"Surely you will have a Ballanlochar? The twenty-four years old, of course, because the others are rubbish."

Of course, who would dare order anything else?

"No sir," said the poor guy apologetically. Suddenly he was deeply interested in his shoes.

"What kind of booze *do* you have?" asked Johnny, cutting to the chase. "It might be easier."

"We have the Jura, the Singleton, the Laphroaig …"

"I'll go for a Laphroaig," said Hugo. "Of course the smokiness is not like that of the Pittighmore, but …"

"Deal!" cut short Johnny, visibly irritated.

"I'll have a full bottle, please," added Hugo as an afterthought.

I looked at my two companions, trying to understand if I was on some sort of candid camera, but no, the situation baffled them as well. Hell, who drinks a bottle of whisky with Indian food?

His ability at gulping down whisky was astonishing; fortunately, the waiter came back for our orders.

"Are you ready to order?"

Hugo, wanting to play the role of the alpha male, ordered a "Chicken Tikka Naga". I had a look at the menu and that came with three huge, fat chillies next to the name. That meant the stuff was really hot. They were serious with their stuff. Three chillies on the menu classified it like a biological weapon. They would use the same ingredients to make the fuel for a nuclear plant. The guys had to have a special licence from the MoD to serve such food and they brought it to the table in the same containers as used to carry radioactive material.

"... and could you add some extra chilli, please?"

"Sir, I would like to warn you that it is already a very hot dish," said the waiter, but Hugo didn't want to hear any of that. The poor chap looked at us, as if we could instil some sense into our friend; after all, we were regulars. I shrugged, Ritchie blabbed something about personal taste, while Johnny said something like, "A curry is never hot enough."

The waiter got the message and gave a devilish smile to all of us. "Very well, sir."

We ordered our food and went back to our conversation, which meant Hugo explaining to us the importance of his work and how he had solved an IT crisis just the night before.

Something that I'd spotted, however, was just how well Ritchie and Johnny were getting along. They'd had only a few dates but were already – what is it that some say? – "in sync". They were so in tune with each other, and that made me incredibly happy. It was about time that Ritchie had some luck in the love department. He laughed so much that evening that I was almost glowing with pleasure on his behalf.

The Indian restaurant was exemplary, at least from my meagre experience. As a whole the evening went well but, as I said, I was not that enamoured with Hugo. I appreciated that Ritchie and Johnny had made an effort and probably filtered out a lot of other men, but – at least once he started talking – I hadn't been that attracted to Hugo either. I couldn't write off the whole evening, though, as we did enjoy ourselves, but I doubted very much that there was going to be a second, mutually agreeable date following that blind one. One last thing, which I had found to be a complete turn-off (far worse than talking about an ex), was that he had been far too familiar with me. To call someone "sweetheart" or "darling", when you've only just met on a first date, was just that little bit too much.

Eventually the food arrived and Hugo attacked his curry. We waited to hear him screaming "hell" but that didn't happen, to our disappointment. We noticed, though, that after every mouthful he gulped down some additional whisky, but somehow we were still disappointed. Perhaps the guy was the real deal and could handle a three-blooming-chilli dish without any trouble.

Then he started sweating.

But it wasn't like when it is a bit warmer and you need to take your jumper off; the guy was sweating as if he were in a sauna. Drops of perspiration were falling profusely from his forehead down his cheeks; he even had some on his nose, ready to drip onto his now empty plate of food.

"I'm sweating ... I can hardly breathe..." he said, and then drank another glass of whisky, finishing the bottle.

Of course you're sweating you moron, I thought; *you've just eaten a chili grenade that could be used to fend off a horde of terrorists.*

"Maybe you need some fresh air," suggested Ritchie.

"Good idea ..." but then, as soon as he got up from his chair, he fell flat on his face, unable to move. It would have been funny if we hadn't been worried that all the chili, coupled with the whisky, could actually have killed him.

But he was alive – and drunk as a skunk. He started blabbering something like, "Thiissssshhh neverrrrr 'appened to me," so, under the concerned look of the other guests, we decided to call him a taxi and end his misery.

"I wouldn't want to be his arse, tomorrow morning," commented Johnny.

"Bloody blimey, for a moment I thought he was dead," laughed Ritchie.

"Where did you find that chap anyway?" I asked him.

Ritchie was in no mood to explain after having paired me with one of the worst dates of my life. "It's a long story" were the only words he uttered, out of embarrassment.

"Well, you're going to spit it out eventually," I said. "Who fancies a beer at the pub around the corner? Ritchie has a big apology to make and he's buying."

The taxi arrived and we had to pour Hugo into it. He collapsed in a huddle on the floor behind the driver's seat; Ritchie, fortunately had Hugo's address.

"Can you take this chap to 25 Wellington Avenue, in Wokingham?"

"Sure, mate, no problem!" answered the cab driver, then he looked at the state of poor Hugo and added, "That'll be twenty quid. And extra if I have to take him into the house."

"Let's settle for twenty quid," said Ritchie, with a smirk on his face.

Hugo muttered something, as if he were trying to apologise for the whole situation.

This was going to be a story we would talk about for some time. Once the taxi had driven off we walked for a while, still exhausted from carrying Hugo, but also in fits of giggles.

"Was it the tequila or the whisky that did the damage?" asked Johnny.

"Dunno, man. Anyway, your taste in restaurants is rubbish. They didn't even have the bloody Fetterthouch Glenghover. Or was the Fetterthouch Ballanlochar? Gee, I sound pissed just by trying to say those names," Ritchie laughed.

"Indeed that is the case; maybe a tad bit too spicy," I added. It was just the two of us against Johnny now.

"Did you see the steam coming out of his ears after the first bite of the Naga?" said Johnny.

We were like schoolgirls who'd seen something naughty that they shouldn't have, seeing what a fool Hugo had made of himself. I, for one, had a picture in my head of the taxi driver dragging Hugo up his path, and either rummaging through his pockets for a key to open his front door and throwing him inside, or just depositing him on his doorstep. I felt sure that Hugo, by that time, would have passed out, leaving him to wake where he lay exposed to the elements.

We all laughed and left and carried on walking, glad Hugo was no longer with us.

CHAPTER 10

As expected, the Bray Saints lost the third match of the season. The mood was as grim as ever; Dex was in mourning and the team was as depressed as a stockbroker during a recession. At least it wasn't raining. I hated to see his team losing that badly and I needed cheering up, so I approached Nala once they had changed. "Fancy a trip into town for some shopping?"

"Hmm … I don't know."

"Don't worry, this trip is just to satisfy my need for new things – to cheer me up. You can just tag along."

"Hmm … sure – why not? Where are we going?"

"I was thinking Windsor; there's a new place a friend of a friend gave me the address of, and I want to check it out. Ever been to Windsor?"

"Just once, with the school; we visited the castle."

"Met our beloved queen?"

"No, nothing like that. We looked at the changing of the guard and then went inside. Lots of paintings, art and stuff."

"Did you like it?"

"Sort of; looked like a fairy-tale palace – I mean living in a castle and stuff."

"Well, this time we go and visit another kind of castle; or to put it better, we're going to do a bit of treasure hunting."

"Do what?" she asked.

"A treasure hunt. We're looking for the perfect outfit."

"For your pleasure or one of your clients?"

"I haven't decided yet," I added, laughing. It was always like that; I never knew for whom I was buying until I saw what I was dealing with. I had to follow the inspiration of the moment and decide on the spot. Not a great strategy, but the only one I knew.

We drove to Windsor and parked not too far from the centre. During the trip I actually learned that Nala could say more than "I don't know," and I found she had a vast range of interests. Football aside, she was a skilled artist. She briefly showed me some of her drawings while we were stuck in traffic and it came as a surprise. She carried a Moleskine block notes and whenever she was in the mood she started drawing. I saw a very nice portrait of Robbie Williams, another one of my brother, and then some others that reminded me of manga cartoons, although there was something more pictorial about them.

"Have you been to this place before?" Nala asked, with a tone in her voice that actually suggested, "Come on, tell me you're lost!"

"Well ... the address is correct, but it's a tatty gift shop; I don't understand," I said. I took her hand and entered. There was nothing that stood out other than the Iron Maiden shirts, and a chubby guy by the till.

"Excuse me – a friend of mine suggested this shop to me, but clearly there was a mistake."

The guy looked me up and down from head to toe and then muttered "Ahhh, a special guest," which sounded very odd.

Then he added, "Who sent you?"

What was that? Next he was going to ask me for a secret password, which I didn't know "Tilly Stephens."

Another look of distrust and then he said, "OK, follow me." He opened a door behind the till and I could see stairs going down. The man invited us to proceed.

"Are you sure about this?" asked Nala.

I wasn't, but what options did I realistically have? Tilly had promised me the holy grail of fashion, and sometimes you have to take a chance. "Sure, no problem," I lied.

After a couple of flights of stairs, the vision before our eyes was incredible. At that very moment I realised how Ali Baba felt when he first entered the forty thieves' den, when Indiana Jones discovered the Ark of the Covenant in the first of his movies, and when Harry finally met Sally. In front of us there was this huge hall, probably an old Victorian warehouse, full of the most enormous array of clothes I had ever come across.

I looked at Nala in order to check

whether she was experiencing nirvana as well, but she just shrugged. Novice!

I could see Jimmy Choos, Armani, Valentino, Roberto Cavalli, Hervé Leger – and those were only the items I could see from the stairs. I thought about it for a second; I have a photographic memory for clothes – even if I see something in a magazine I'll remember it – but some of those clothes were new to me, although I recognised the style.

"Where has all this stuff come from?" I asked the ogre who accompanied us.

"Young lady, the rules are that you look around, you try what you want, and if you want to take something home, you pay at the till. No questions asked."

"Hmmm ..."

"And no, there are no stolen items in here."

"Hmmm ..."

"And no, we're not selling cheap Chinese copies, or any other type of copy for that matter. Everything you see is original, branded and legitimate." Then he waved his hand in the general direction of the clothes racks and added, "Have fun, ladies." Well, I guessed conversation time was over and hunting time had just begun.

"Oh my gosh! This is a Hervé Leger, and the rack says "samples". Do you know what that means?" I asked Nala. She did not; she was looking at me, baffled, as if I was speaking an alien language. "Oh, don't worry," I said, grabbing a couple of outfits, "just follow my lead."

We were ready for battle. At least I was; my companion would have to tag along.

I tried on a navy ruched Ted Baker blouse that was just adorable, with a black pinstripe running through it. The fabric was like a seersucker, but not quite, as it felt more like silk. I coupled that with a pair of black Gant jeans which fit just like a glove. Nala was more interested in browsing and taking in the names of the designers and, of course, checking out the prices.

"Come on, trying doesn't cost anything; worst case is you go back to the Goths. You might actually find something in here as well," I said, looking around the treasure den. "What about this? – just amuse me for once." Nala shook her head and carried on browsing.

She knew she had little or no money, and she might still be at school, with her parents coming from a working-class background, but I could see that she was enthralled. It was as though she were in a trance, especially once she saw the prices and having decided that, maybe, just maybe, I was going to treat her to one of those glorious outfits. Suddenly she stopped dead in her tracks and just stood there staring, her eyes just about as wide as they could be. She was in front of a rail of dresses, of a style that was more suited to her age. There was a red-and-white checked mini-dress, which had frills and flowers, and. I was surprised that she was gawping at it, almost with her tongue hanging out like a thirsty dog. Nala had not struck me as the type of person that would like frills etc., especially with her usual Gothic-style attire. I edged forward slowly, so as not to make her jump out of her skin; she was so intent on staring at that dress. I gently leaned past her, removed the dress from the rail, checked the size and price and handed it to her. She just stood there, transfixed.

Nala grabbed the article, went into a changing room after a bit of huffing and puffing; when she returned wearing the dress, despite having all her Gothic make-up still on, all I could do was whistle and clap my hands. "What do you think?" I asked.

"It looks good. I like it," she said, "but I can hardly afford it."

"Oh, don't worry about that; you don't have to buy it. I just wanted to show you there are other ways to stand out from the crowd, other than being a Goth."

"I suppose so."

Nala did a little twirl and went to have a look in the full-length mirror by the side of the dressing room. I had the suspicion that I might have just succeeded in converting her away from Goth, and possibly the black make-up as well. She looked stunning in that dress.

"Next stop, we'll go to TK Maxx and another couple of places, and you'll see that, with the right combination, you can wear something interesting without breaking the bank," I said. Funnily enough, I rarely managed to do that myself.

CHAPTER 11

The once-growing customer list had dropped to zero and we needed to do something about it or we'd soon have been in trouble. I also took a step towards my independence and rented a small apartment in the centre of Camberley. The good news was that I now had a walk-in wardrobe; the bad news was that the walk-in wardrobe filled the whole apartment. Actually, I had placed every possible hanger and cloth rail in any available space and now it looked as though I was living in my own personal shop. There was a bed, of course, but in order to reach it I had to move all the clothes and boxes of shoes I'd temporarily parked on it.

But it was mine and that was what mattered. In addition, Ritchie and the Hulk were going great guns and I honestly felt they deserved a bit more privacy. Ritchie never said a word and to be honest I thought he was glad I was around, but I also knew he wouldn't have said anything anyway. And then, it was time to move on. We agreed to use his apartment as our place of work, for which I was extremely grateful, as renting an office would have been too risky considering how erratic our revenue was. There were the rich customers coming along with hefty pay, and then possibly a month of emptiness, without a single client or enquiry. That was the difficult part, knowing we would soon need the money but not knowing if another customer would show up. Every day was a battle to keep our dream alive and not go back to our previous employment. But that was what they always said in *Dragon's Den*: you have to have vision and be enthusiastic about your venture. Or something like that.

Anyway, Camberley it was, although I would definitely have preferred Windsor. That afternoon was as empty as a hermit's address book, so I decided I needed to get out for some fresh air. The destination was the Oracle Centre in Reading – nothing really glamorous, but that day they had a small market taking place and I could waste a few hours trying to think of a new strategy to grow my business.

That event happened exactly two hours and twenty minutes later when I entered a Rascal & Brody shop, one of my favourite destinations, at least as far as shoes were concerned. As soon as I entered, all the shop assistants ran away: one became suddenly busy taking away boxes of shoes, another one picked up a phone which wasn't ringing, near the cash register, and pretended to be speaking with another customer. The third one just panicked and ran away as if she were being chased by the devil himself.

I looked at my clothes and they were OK; I couldn't understand. Then I sniffed my armpits: no bad odour there either. I was wearing a hat, so it couldn't have been my hair.

"It's not you, it's me," I heard a voice echoing behind me. I turned around and saw a tall, handsome man in his thirties, with short, dark hair. He was wearing a pair of black trousers and seemed in good shape, albeit a bit on the slim side.

"They don't like you?"

"I think not. I buy women's shoes and every time it's the same story: they just disappear. I'm lucky if I can find the right size, otherwise I have to beg for attention."

Inevitably, I looked at his feet, but he was wearing a pair of black loafers, and maybe the only thing wrong was that they were a bit boring. "For yourself or for someone else?"

"Oh, they'll be for me."

I picked up a bit of embarrassment in his voice, so I promptly extended my hand and said, "I'm GiGi, by the way."

"My pleasure, GiGi; I'm Julian."

"Nice to meet you. Let's see what we can do about that pair of shoes. What's your style?"

"Sexy. Definitely sexy."

"OK, Julian – what size do you wear?"

"I'm a perfect eight, darling," he said, with a broad smile on his face.

"I bet you are." I caught the attention of one of the shop assistants and barked a few orders to her, which she gladly complied with. After a few seconds they came out with their best offerings. Julian tried a few pairs, walking up and down the shop and attracting some weird looks. I was one of them; I mean, a tall bloke in purple pumps had to attract attention.

I looked around for something suitable for myself, but nothing really caught my eye so I went back to Julian. "How's it going?"

"I look fabulous; what do you think?"

"You certainly do."

"Would you mind sticking around for a few more minutes, at least until I've paid?" he added sheepishly "I could reward you with a cup of coffee. Not the cheap stuff, I mean a real coffee like the ones they have down in Avangard."

"I'd be glad to."

Julian gave a last look at his marvellous shoes, put his loafers back on and said, "OK, let's get out of here and put an end to the show."

I followed him to the cashier, waited until he had paid and then we set off walking towards the coffee shop. I had never been there previously and to my surprise it was a very classy shop – I mean, with real napkins and proper cutlery; it almost resembled a restaurant. "Is the place to your liking?"

"It certainly is," I answered. We sat at a corner table by the window and I asked, "What kind of business are you in, Julian?"

"Oh, I work for the local council here in Reading. I'm a bin man, although today they use the more politically correct term of waste collector."

"Yeah, let's not go to the politically correct; I lose the plot nowadays. So where do the shoes fit in?" I asked.

The waiter came and Julian ordered coffee for two, adding some pastries for good measure.

"They don't, actually. The pay isn't great, so I round my salary up doing some gigs in London. My drag act is quite popular and I make more money over the weekend than in my day job."

"A drag act in London? I've never heard of anything like that."

"Yeah, there are a couple of venues; one is the Pegasus, Friday nights, in the West End. It's quite popular among people who like to wear dresses; they even have a changing room. If you go in there unnoticed a couple of hours before the show, you can change and sort out your make-up and there you go: you can be a queen for the night."

"So they're all in drag?" I asked, feeling my curiosity mounting.

"No, there are the drags and there are the admirers. The latter dress normally, although I have to admit with far less taste. And then there's the Oriental, on Thursdays and Saturdays. That's a real wild place."

"What's your act?"

"It's me and three other 'girls'; we mostly sing and dance. We lip-sync to the most famous songs, we dance, and we tease the public a bit. It's getting more popular, and it's a safe place where someone can express their real self without being judged or risking a beating in the street."

"Makes sense."

"And what do you do, GiGi, for a living?"

"At the moment I struggle; however, I'm a personal shopper."

"Meaning?"

"I go around and buy clothes on behalf of someone else. I've also started recently as a fashion consultant, so I can give advice to people on what to wear and how to avoid the most common mistakes."

That made Julian ponder, and once the waiter brought our coffees and had moved far enough away, he spoke again.

"I have this problem in buying outfits for my show; I mean, I find it embarrassing sometimes, not only with the shoes but also with the clothes, wigs and so on. You know, having to try them on; some of the looks I get you cannot imagine. I'm a fury when on stage and I'm unstoppable, but when I have to go into a shop, like today, I freeze."

"Well, Julian, you'd better get used to it, gather all the courage you're capable of and just embrace your inner self. Things might change in the future, but there's still discrimination if you're homosexual. The only way is to ignore all that and live your life as you wish, without fear of judgement. The longer you delay, the unhappier you're going to be."

"I think you misunderstood me: I'm not gay, I'm straight. The drag job is only to pay the bills and I'm good at that. I mean, I'm a regular guy with no particular talent, but when I dress up and act, I feel I have something to give, even if it is a Saturday-night show. It's difficult to explain."

"I think I get it …" I said.

And then Julian had an idea. "Would you help me? I mean, if you're a personal shopper, that would make things easier.. You could buy on my behalf."

I wasn't expecting that, although it made perfect sense. How many people out there were facing the same struggle as Julian?

"So you want me to buy clothes on your behalf?"

"I think so: why not?"

"I guess I might have to see one of your shows, to have an idea of what might fit the profile."

"I have a few on YouTube. Wanna take a peek?"

He took out his phone and showed me a few clips of his performances. I could understand why he preferred that to the bin-man job; he and his team were definitely talented. Dancing, singing, the occasional joke that made people laugh. He was up to something, but most of all I was interested in their outfits. They had to be sexy, tempting and seductive. I guess my imagination could have gone a tad wild and, for once, I wouldn't be bound to the classic style. I had the chance to be outrageous.

"I think I could do something about that." I passed him one of my business cards. "I'd like you to send me some of those clips for reference. What sort of budget did you have in mind?"

He gave me a number and, after a quick calculation, I said, "I can work with that."

"I mean monthly – I need a lot of outfits. I can't go on stage with the same stuff over and over again."

Bloody blimey, I was in the wrong business. I thought about asking why he still stuck to his day job, but I stopped myself. I said out loud, "OK, so maybe to keep down costs we need some sort of 'rental' agreement. Instead of buying all the clothes,

I can try to figure out if we could sell the old ones; in that way you'd have more choices for the same price."

"That would be fabulous!" He gave me his phone number.

"I'll be in touch shortly, then."

Dear old GiGi, you're back in business, I thought.

CHAPTER 12

The news came as a surprise.

"Afghanistan? When, how, why?" I was completely shocked. It was a bright morning, the world was my oyster and business seemed to be back on track and, although not flying high, there was enough to pay rent and bills. I went to the office – well, actually Ritchie's apartment – full of renewed energy, only to find him sitting in the kitchen and staring at his empty cup of tea. I soon learned what was wrong.

"He told me the news yesterday; in a week he'll be gone for a six-month tour. He'd been hoping it was either going to be postponed or put off altogether."

My dearest friend was really upset and, as usual, he started biting his nails; if I couldn't cheer him up, he'd bite them until they were bleeding. But where to start? I could hardly try to comfort him, other than giving him a hug. I was speechless. What could I say?

Reading the papers and following politics were not my forte; the furthest I went on news was around fashion, but there was an entire world out there that needed sorting out and I could barely comprehend why our country was sending our beloved soldiers so far away. Don't get me wrong: I knew the war in Afghanistan was to try to dismantle al-Qaeda and remove the Taliban from power down there. I could understand all the reasons why our country was doing that, but somehow it was just something I was hearing in the news, as far and distant from my little world of clothes and fashion as it could possibly be.

War.

It had been in the news for quite a while, but I never really thought about it and in some respects I carried on doing my thing and just being occasionally upset when I was watching the evening news on telly. That is, until someone I really knew had to go there.

That was a real wake-up call; suddenly our military presence in a foreign country, very far away from our shores, was a personal business – something that touched me, and most of all my very close, treasured friend.

What can you really say when something like that happens? You try to recollect what you've heard, why it was so important that our military went there, the fight against terrorism; but the fear for someone you knew personally who was going to be out there, in constant danger, was overwhelming.

Then comes the need for protection - all the silly questions like *Can he avoid that? Is there a way for him not to go?* And suddenly you also know you already have the answer to the questions. That something is unavoidable, that Johnny wouldn't let us interfere in it anyway, even if we had a chance. That was his choice; he had decided to serve our country, even if that meant risking his own life. Suddenly, our little problems about paying the rent, finding the next customer, doing a good job, became even more insignificant in comparison to that.

We sat there in the kitchen, in silence, and I also started to stare at my cup of coffee, mulling over the meaning of the news.

"Six months, you said?"

"Yes, six damn' long months," he said, still looking into his mug. "It isn't the time that bothers me – I can wait six months, no problem. It's that I fear I'll spend every day of those six months worrying that he might be in danger, that something might happen to him. And then I'll spend the night doing the same."

"Is there a way of staying in touch? I mean by phone or text?"

"Apparently there is this company Skype, which allows making calls through the computer; that could be a way. I have to look into that."

"But … do they have broadband in Afghanistan? How will it work?"

"They have computers at the base camp and they should be able to send emails and perhaps use this Skype too."

"That's not so bad then. A bit of a long-distance relationship."

"I suppose so. So who do we have to save

from fashion disaster today?" he asked. I was glad we were going back into work mode, as I really didn't know what more I could have said about the whole military situation.

"Well, we have Julian and his stage outfits; we have the lady from Sunningdale, whose husband has agreed to foot the bill; and then there's that divorcee from Bray." Enough to keep us busy for a while.

"And your pet project with Nala, the footballer."

"That one as well, but it won't pay the rent. I'm particularly struggling with Julian: I've got the style and the budget, but although it's going to be OK it won't be fabulous," I said.

"And that bothers you why? The guy asked you to buy clothes, not to change his style."

"I know, but it's like a leaking tap; I can't stop thinking I should be doing something more." Ritchie, as usual, was right: I should have stuck to the plan.

"What do you have in mind?"

"I was thinking, you have a few friends

who are fashion designers, don't you?"

He mulled it over and then answered, "Of course, but the question remains, what do you have in mind?"

"Maybe – and this is just a maybe – we could have someone create his outfits; it might be an opportunity."

"Hmm ..." Ritchie was pondering, started biting his nails again and then changed his mind. Instead, he went for another cup of tea. When he came back I knew something was going on in his mind.

"Do you remember my cousin Lucas?" he asked.

"The one that works for Rocco Barocco?"

"That very one. Why don't you give him a call? I remember a few months back he said he was bored stiff designing shirts. Maybe he can help, or knows somebody that could."

That was actually a great idea, having a real designer doing costumes. From what Julian had said, they had to last for a few shows only; he didn't need to wear them all the time, so perhaps that could be a viable option. "Where do I find his number?"

"It's on the computer, under Cousin Lucas; the chap never had a surname."

We both laughed; I had some relatives like that, Auntie Anna and Uncle James, for example. I knew everything about them, we got in touch often by phone, but if someone asked me for their surnames I'd have been lost.

"I'll give him a call right away. You'll take care of the lady in Sunningdale?"

"Sure, I'm working on some ideas; I'll show you later."

And so I went and called Cousin Lucas. As a matter of fact, he said he did hate being stuck just designing shirts and he would welcome the opportunity for a new "adventure", as he called it. He giggled a bit when he heard about how my new client, the council worker, rounded up his salary, but it took only a few words to bring him in line.

"So I can really do whatever I want?" he asked, surprised.

"I've just sent you a couple of links to his Youtube videos. Have a good look and, as long as you understand what his job is and how magnificent he has to appear, you should be OK."

"That would be brilliant, GiGi. I was thinking, quite often companies send me samples of their fabrics, just in case we want to use them in our models. In reality we don't, as we just produce our own things, but nonetheless I get all these leftovers and fabric. I haven't the heart to throw them away, so I keep storing them at my place. I could use some of those ..."

"As I said, you're free to follow your inspiration; just don't go mad. I guess a couple of designs would be more than enough to start, just to see his reaction. If he likes them, then we're in business."

"I will. Thank you, GiGi; you've made my day."

"A pleasure, Cousin Lucas; see you soon."

I was on the verge of asking his surname, but then I thought otherwise. Some things are better when they remain unknown.

It was late in the afternoon when I received a text from Nala.

– Fashion emergency! Help!!!

Nala? What could be that urgent to convince her to text me? I answered back.

– *Meet me @ the pub in 1 hour.*

The reply came after a few seconds.

– *Cool. Thx.*

I was pretty much sorted out for the day, so I left Ritchie at his own research, and surely he'd like to … damn! How could I have been so stupid? Of course he'd like to spend time with Johnny, so before I went out I said, "Ritchie, for this week take as much time off as you need, especially if you need to see Johnny. Don't worry about the lady in Sunningdale – I can pick it up where you've left it."

"Are you sure? I mean …"

"Yeah, of course I'm OK with that. Spend as much time with him as you need. Those are the important things: work can wait."

"Thanks, GiGi; I really appreciate that."

"Don't mention it."

CHAPTER 13

I reached the pub and Nala seemed somehow prettier. It took me a full minute to realise she wasn't in full Goth mode: I saw less tatty clothes, an attempt to sort out her hair and less make-up. I was glad she'd dumped the dark lipstick, which made her look like a witch. They would have burned her at the stake a few centuries ago, just for looking the way she had previously.

"Hi there. What's the emergency?"

She was embarrassed for sure; I could spot that a mile away.

"Well, how should I say …? D'you remember the place we went to together in Windsor?"

Duh? The holy grail of affordable fashion? The Ali Baba cave? "Yes, of course I remember."

"Well, I was in Windsor with my mum and you know, I really liked that dress we saw together."

"The expensive one?"

"Yeah, that one. So I said to my mum there was this dress I liked. At first she thought I was going after some other Goth stuff, but then eventually I convinced her to go and have a look."

Hmmm ... maybe I was seeing, in front of my very eyes, the symptoms of a conversion. Was I detecting a radical change in her approach to her looks? Who knew that the road to Damascus was through Windsor?

She continued, "So, we went downstairs and I showed her the dress. You should have seen the look on her face. At first her jaw dropped as if she'd just seen an alien in front of her. Then she almost cried, sobbing, 'Oh, my little baby' as if I was a lost sheep finally returning home. It was pathetic. But she bought me the dress."

Still I was missing the point, so I invited her to carry on.

"Oh, yes," she answered, "the other day I went to this party that Bridge was having for her birthday, and Bradley was there."

"Who's Bradley?" Blimey, this was going

to be a long story, I feared. If Dan Brown should run out of inspiration for one of his novels, I could present Nala to him. Fifty–fifty split in revenue.

"Oh, Bradley is a guy who goes to my school."

"And you fancy him?"

"Yeah, but he's never given me a second glance. I mean, I've tried to talk to him a few times; he's polite and all but …"

"But he doesn't fancy you back."

"Something like that."

"Sorry, Nala – today I'm a bit on the dumb side. Why has this anything to do with a fashion emergency?" I was starting to get confused; I had my iron in too many fires at once and barely time to sort out all the things I needed to take care of. Clients, friendships, fashion disasters …

"Oh, yes, sure. Well, I went to the party wearing that dress and Bradley was all over me. I mean, he was chatty, funny, and he approached ME, not the other way round. Bottom line is, we have a date lined up."

OK, now we were getting to the fashion-emergency issue. She liked the guy, but she couldn't go out again with him for a date wearing the same dress, and if things were to go any further she needed a change of style. Oh, the things we do for love …

"And you need some new outfits, so he won't be scared away."

"That's right. Can you help me, GiGi? Pleeease?"

"Of course I can, but first we have to do 'the ritual'," I said.

"The WHAT?"

"The ritual. It's serious. Shalt thou, Nala, repent and abandon the evil path of Goth?" I said solemnly.

She looked at me as if I was out of my mind, but then she answered "Hmmm …I … shall?"

"Good. Wilt thou, Nala, embrace the world of fashion and abide by the sacred rule of colour matching?"

"I … will?" she said tentatively.

"Shalt thou reject the old saying, 'Blue and green should never be seen'?" I continued. That was a favourite saying of my mother.

"GiGi, are you taking the mickey?"

"I ammmmm," I said, chanting, and then we burst out laughing.

"You are a character."

"Sometimes, but when it's a matter of fashion, I'm very serious. So what did you have in mind?"

"Well, Mum gave me a prepaid card. And that's where I stopped in my planning. Oh, she had some ruling attached to this," Nala said, showing me the brand-new card. "For every item of clothing that I buy and bring into the house, a Goth one has to leave."

"Wise woman. Are you happy with that?"

"I don't mind, as long as it lands me more dates with Bradley."

"Well then, we have a deal. We'll start tomorrow afternoon after you've finished school. I'll have to ponder where to take you and what style might suit you."

The day had come for Johnny to depart. I hadn't seen Ritchie in a week and when he turned up, bleary-eyed, his face was a picture. His eyes were sullen and sunken. He'd obviously been crying, having seen

Johnny off at some unearthly hour of the morning. I made a quick decision to try and take his mind off the heart-wrenching fact that, unless he could get the new Skype thing working, he wouldn't be seeing Johnny for six months or so. My plan was to find out how their week together had been, given that Johnny had had to spend a good deal of that time preparing to leave.

It was time for me to plug him for information on Johnny.

"Here, take these," I said, slipping the pastries on the table in his direction and pouring fresh coffee under his nose.

"Thanks, GiGi."

"So, did you manage to sort out that Skype account?"

"Yeah, I sorted it out," he paused for a second and then added, "I can't believe he's going!"

"Not for long, Ritchie; he'll be back. How was the week?" I enquired.

"Fabulous. The first night we stayed at home, dinner by candlelight, followed by a soppy film and accessories …"

"Accessories?!"

"Relax, darling: it was just chocolate and champagne."

"OK, I thought you were going commando."

"That came later; want to know the details?" he prodded me.

"Hmmm, no, you can spare me that. So, champagne and chocolate – then what?" I said.

"The usual stuff grown-up people do; we learned every inch of our bodies, we …"

"Enough said! I was looking for the romantic bit, to be honest, not a lesson in anatomy."

"Can't have one without the other, darling," he laughed. Ritchie had such a smirk on his face while recounting that night that it obviously had had some effect.

"OK, then what? Don't tell me you stayed in bed the whole week; that sounds too much like *Barefoot in the Park*." I said

"Darling, we're not cavemen; we went to a music festival. Johnny had bought the tickets just after we met. I love the guy. Well, I suppose it was an investment; they were hard to find, you know?"

"I bet they were; only the best for a catch like you," I teased him.

"Yeah, sure; say what you want, but Johnny is a true gentleman. We were still buzzing at two in the morning that night. We had to walk home because we couldn't find a taxi. But I like to remember it as a long meander along the Thames by moonlight."

"That sounds exciting."

"Not like the day after. We were both exhausted, so we stayed in bed. There it is; that could be classified as an attempt to do our own *Barefoot in the Park*. The first part of the movie, at least."

"I love that."

"It was, although then he went to his parents' place. He made a point of wanting to remember all the tastes of home before going off to such a faraway country."

The more I heard the story from Ritchie, the more I grew fond of Johnny. He was indeed a good guy, despite his menacing appearance.

"One thing made an impression on me," said Ritchie.

"What's that?"

"He said than when he was at his parents, he made them repeat all the family stories they could remember – the things they did when he was a child, about the grandparents and so on. He wanted that to help him to keep a connection alive between them during the six months that he's going to be away," he said.

"I can't even imagine what it would be like spending six months in Afghanistan," I said, "especially under these conditions, with the war and all."

"Indeed."

"At least you have a chance to talk to him, which is absolutely brilliant," I said.

"I do hope it isn't going to be too hard. I mean, once you're there, you're at war."

Ritchie then went through the details of the following days, and how on the Monday Johnny had had to return to base to begin his preparations.

I saw that the more Ritchie talked, and as their week together had drawn to a close, the more his sense of loss returned.

"All I could think about was that if this is what it's like now, and Johnny hadn't even set off yet, how I was going to feel when he went away for six months," said Ritchie.

They saw each other on and off during the week and on the Saturday morning Ritchie had awoken to breakfast in bed, red rose and all. Johnny had gone the whole hog and made eggs benedict, completely from scratch, including the hollandaise sauce. He had coupled that with crispy bacon, toast and Buck's Fizz (not the plain old boring one, though – this one he'd made with apricot juice). They had then spent the morning at the gym, had lunch at one of those little bistros with tables on the pavement, and returned to Ritchie's just in time to prepare dinner.

Ritchie said, "We were both so solemn, you'd have thought we'd each lost a close friend or relative."

They had then spent the rest of the time in bed, until the following early-morning start, which had been tearful, especially as they had to do it secretly. The Army was still not all that enamoured with its officers being gay.

CHAPTER 14

Sorting out Nala was an easy task and the results were astonishing. Not only did she look really pretty in her new attire, but the dates with Bradley were going well and at some point she texted me, letting me know they were together.

I didn't need the news, as I'd spotted him myself when he regularly showed up at the Bray Saints' matches. Nala also showed much more determination, both during the football matches and outside, and she soon became a catalyst for the rest of the team – a true leader. She started bonding with them; she had a witty sense of humour that somehow she'd kept hidden until then and, most of all, to the joy and happiness of my brother, the team started winning.

We also paid a visit to an old friend of mine, a hair stylist who owed me a favour and who gave Nala a new look.

I received a thank-you card from her

mother and, sure enough, I made it onto their Christmas-card list too. I was glad for her, because the first time I'd seen her she didn't really strike me as a happy bunny – she was lost in trying to build or find a personality that she didn't know was already in her. I wouldn't say I did anything much, but I think I helped her to see her inner self, to become more confident and open. That was an achievement I'd carry with me for the rest of my life.

On the work side, the other clients were also happy.

In particular, Julian. Eventually I was able to show him a couple of samples from Cousin Lucas, and he was amazed. I found him a new wardrobe of things to wear during his show, and he was ecstatic. However, it was clear enough to me that Cousin Lucas had struck a chord in him. Those designs were fabulous, sexy, intriguing and, from that point onwards, that was it: Lucas would be the master designer, the one and only to dress Julian.

The results were impressive; after the show many people asked him who was the source of that fantastic change and Julian, not willing to spill the beans about Cousin Lucas, directed them to me. That gave me a few additional clients.

I could just imagine my mother's face if I told her about my new set of customers, and had to laugh. "Hello, Mum – I'm the official fashion consultant for the drag queens in London; d'you fancy coming and seeing a show next Saturday?"

That would have raised a few eyebrows, but business was business and that was a challenge I honestly couldn't give up. On the other hand; what was worrying me was Ritchie.

A few weeks had passed since the last message with Johnny and he was starting to get twitchy. At first he went into drama mode, imagining all sorts of accident and even fearing the worst, which kept him awake for a few nights.

Then he went into a different mood, thinking that maybe Johnny had dumped him and didn't want to face him. That was complete rubbish, and I let him know he was being a horse's arse about that.

"Come on, Ritchie; from what I know of Johnny he's not the type to shy away from a relationship. He's better than that and if he'd wanted to break up, he would have said something."

"Yeah, but it's been a few weeks; I don't know what else to think."

"Did you try to call him?"

"Yes, I'm online nearly all the time, even at night, but he's not showing up on Skype. And his mobile doesn't work down there. I even tried sending emails, but haven't received any answers."

"Maybe he's involved in some sort of mission? We don't really know what's going on there and surely they might have some difficult times. Enough not to be back at camp or able to sit at the computer."

"I also tried some friends we have in common," he added, "but they haven't heard anything either."

I didn't know what to think and Ritchie was useless in that state, so I said, "Take the day off. I'll go and work from my apartment. And relax – I'm sure it's nothing to worry about."

"Thanks, GiGi."

And so I went home; after all, I needed a break from work as well – but something was nagging me. I opened Facebook and started searching; I knew Johnny wasn't there; he wasn't the Facebook type, but maybe I could find a way to get to some close friends? I started from his regiment, but there was nothing; then I remembered he had a sister called Jennifer. With a surname like his, Jones, that was a losing battle though.

Maybe there was a way of calling his battalion in the UK to see if I could get through that way? I started searching the internet and my heart sank. A few links were showing an association between his battalion and a Johnny Jones, killed in action.

It couldn't have been!

The more I read, the more I was convinced that the worst had actually happened and Johnny was dead. In particular, there was an article from the local paper showing a picture of the deceased soldier and mentioning his bravery. Damn! The article was a week old and none of us had spotted it. I was engrossed in my job and dear Ritchie … well, he wasn't exactly a news person. I kept reading and later they showed a picture of the parents; Johnny had been their only son. They lived not far from Camberley and I was wondering if they knew their son was gay.

I searched the directory and found the address straight away. *Maybe I should pay them a visit and see what they said before breaking the news to Ritchie,* I thought. Oh gosh, how many doubts that brought. What if they didn't know about Ritchie? Maybe he should have been the one to talk to them first but, if he was going to burst into tears, would he be able to keep his composure?

That decided it: I would have to meet the parents and give them my condolences. I wrote down the address and I started sobbing. I knew that guy; he was funny and lovely. He had lost his life fighting for our country and now he was no more. What would the pain be like that his family would have to endure, and Ritchie as well, if I already felt that empty?

I bashed a fist on the table, cursing the government for letting him go to Afghanistan and die like that, but that wasn't the point, I said to myself. Johnny had made a choice, to serve his country and help to protect all of us here at home, so we could carry on living our lives and enjoying our freedom. I felt useless and all my little efforts to make the world "a better place" seemed at that point so empty, without any value in comparison to his ultimate sacrifice.

Poor Johnny.

But I had to visit his parents, without further ado, and pay my respects. I didn't know what I was going to say and I was afraid I'd burst into tears again; but it was the right thing to do. So I went to my car and, after a few minutes spent drying my eyes, I started the engine.

The house was a semi-detached, like many others around. There was a small garden with a red Japanese maple in the middle. At the front was an empty driveway, which made me wonder if the

Joneses were at home, but I parked nonetheless and, after a long sigh, I rang the doorbell.

A lady in her mid-fifties came to open the door. I tried to see if I could identify the pain she was enduring, but I could see only a pair of sad eyes looking at me.

"Yes?" she asked me.

"Mrs Jones, I'm sorry to bother you, but I recently learned the news about Johnny. I wanted to extend my condolences to you and your husband."

She suddenly looked ten years older at the mention of his name, and then she whispered, "Thank you."

I stayed there, with nothing else to say, for a few seconds, afraid I would start crying. Almost as an afterthought, Mrs Jones said, "Do you want to come in?"

"Thank you."

The lounge was fairly large and sitting in an armchair was the husband, reading a newspaper. He rose and shook my hand.

"So you knew Johnny?"

"Yes, I did. He was a brave man."

"We miss him so much. Had you known

him for long?"

"No, not really: just for the past six or seven months, but he'd made a big impression. He was so jovial, and as far I knew he seemed a happy person."

"He was, although it hadn't always been like that," said his mother; then she went to a table where a few photos were standing, and gestured to me to come closer. She showed me pictures of Johnny in his childhood, and where they were taken, and then other, later ones after he'd joined the Army.

"You know, we still kept his room as it was. Occasionally he came to visit and spend the night here. It was as though our family was together again, even for a little while."

We spent a few more minutes talking about him and I thanked God I hadn't started crying, although I'd had to make a huge effort not to. I knew that if I had tears in my eyes the parents would start crying as well and I wanted to avoid that. In that tragic situation I wanted to pass on the message that Johnny had been loved, that I wanted to remember him when he'd been happy. It was soon time to depart and Mrs Jones accompanied me to the door. I kissed her on the cheek and when I started walking towards my car, as an afterthought she said, "Do you know, by any chance, a guy called Ritchie Garrett?"

My blood froze in my veins. "I … as a matter of fact, yes I do."

"We know Johnny was very fond of him; he always talked about Ritchie when he was around."

"So, you knew …"

"Of course we knew, but we didn't know how to contact Ritchie."

I had to tell her that Ritchie didn't know the news yet – that I had just found out that day and had come there straight away.

"We really would like to meet him, and if he could say a few words at the funeral, we'd be so grateful."

We exchanged numbers, with the promise to get in touch. Now I had to deliver some very bad news to my dearest friend.

CHAPTER 15

It was a disaster.

How do you break the news to someone that his beloved one has just died? At first came the denial, the reluctance to understand that what I'd told him was true, and the hope that maybe there had been a mistake and the news, somehow, was wrong. Then it started to sink in and it felt as if his life, all of a sudden, had become empty.

And then, only then, did he start to feel the pain and the loss.

Ritchie went through all these phases, and I with him. We cried together, we hugged and then cried a bit more. Eventually I told him about my visit to Johnny's parents and that shook him a bit. He was in no condition to go and see them straight away, but he promised me he would do that the following day.

I went home that night feeling as empty

as a shell.

I had never faced death before. I mean, I'd had some long-distant relatives who had died previously, but I was somehow detached from them. They were people I'd barely known, who were mentioned once in a while by my parents, but I'd never suffered the loss of one so close to me, someone who'd been a part of my life, although indirectly; someone who "I knew".

How do you cope with that? I couldn't; I didn't know what to do or think, and I felt completely useless. Eventually, Ritchie went to visit the Joneses and gained some relief from that meeting. We never spoke about the occasion or what they'd said to each other; the only thing I knew was my old friend let slip "that he had acquired a new set of parents". We left it at that.

For a few weeks I didn't show up at his apartment for work, but spent most of my time in my own place and making the occasional visit to clients.

It came as a surprise when he decided that he didn't want to live in his place any longer; we met a few times at the pub and eventually he spilled the beans. Every time he was at home he was thinking of Johnny and he couldn't find a way of getting out of that loop, so eventually he went back to live with his parents.

I couldn't blame him; I'd probably have done the same if I were in his position. People react to this sort of thing in different ways and Ritchie was withdrawing into himself. From my apartment/walk-in wardrobe I thought many times about what I should have done or said, but every time I thought of something I soon found thousands of arguments that told me otherwise. Eventually I settled for "just being there", going out for lunch or for a beer and waiting.

They say that time heals all wounds, but I hadn't seen any sign of that, and at the end of the day I thought it was just a saying, a big pile of rubbish. I would never forget Johnny and I'd never forget the pain I felt when I heard the news, but that would be only a fraction of what Ritchie had been feeling.

I kept paying him his salary, hoping that one day he would come to accept, somehow, that life has to go on, even if sometimes – often – it stinks.

And then one evening, out of nowhere, when we were having dinner at his parents' house, he said, "Do you need any research done?"

That was the first time, in over two months, that he'd mentioned work; I almost jumped out of my chair and ran to hug him. I hoped we could re-establish our working relationship as it had been before, as we were a great team.

"Sure, I have plenty."

"I don't have my place any more, but Dad said we could use the shed. Unless you prefer working in your tiny apartment, that is."

I didn't have a chance in hell of swinging a cat there, what with all my clothes and stuff lying around; contemplating fitting a couple of desks in as well was out of the question. "In the shed?"

"Yeah, the big one. We cleaned it up this past weekend and it's quite big. It even has windows."

"In the shed?" I asked again.

"Well, we could run a cable extension, you know, for the computers, and maybe a heater. I also saw in PC World that there's a piece of equipment that would give us wireless as well …"

"Do we have space for a couple of desks?"

"Plenty. Actually only for one, but it could be a large one, to share. And then you're often away to visit customers, so we could …"

"Relax, Ritchie; you've sold it to me!" I said.

He jumped out of his chair and came around the table to hug me "Thank you, GiGi; you'll love it!"

"Wait and see the backlog I have, and then I think you may regret your thanks."

"I don't mind. I have so much to catch up on, I'll work night and day."

"There's no need for that."

The following weekend I went to look at the shed, or "the office" as we started to call it.

We had a tiny electric heater, more cable extensions and plugs than any person with common sense would have allowed in a wooden structure, but it was "home".

The Bray Saints didn't win the championship, but they made the middle of the list, making my brother a happy bunny. Nala was the captain and now in full control of her destiny, shaping the team with Dex and laying the basis for a stronger team the following year. Her date, Bradley, become her boyfriend, while I had Ritchie back and a decent-sized business that was growing.

Who knew? – one day we might be big enough to take London by storm; but at that point, I admit, I was only daydreaming.

******

I just wanted to say thank you for purchasing this my novel.

Before you go off and hunt for your next great read I would very much appreciate you leaving feedback on the website you purchased it from.

More from this author…

Blue and Green Should Never be Seen!

(or so Mother says)

COLETTE KEBELL

CHAPTER 1

Norwegian jumpers for Christmas? Oh, come off it! I do have some ethics, after all.

This guy is driving me nuts.

You might think the decline started in 2008, when the recession hit us all, but actually no. The BIG problem started when I decided I could improve the world by expanding my business. Adding a male section to my personal shopping website seemed the right thing to do at that time. After all, why limit my expertise to only half of the world? I was wrong – no, I was deeply wrong, on so many levels.

At first people thought, unbelievably and for whatever reason, that it was a dating website and spammed me. "Hey, is it you in that picture?" or, even worse, "What size are you?" Among those, there was the odd genuine person who would have benefited from some style advice. But let's be frank: they were only a few. Despite my polite answers (after all, I am a Personal Shopper) I soon realised there was no hope.

The latest request, received today, was from a Jasper Barnes, allegedly working as an entrepreneur in London, asking me to find him a Norwegian jumper. Size was included in the email. Personally, I don't have anything against Norwegian jumpers. Some of them are beautiful. My best friends wear them. The problem is how to explain to a grown-up man that those sweaters make you look like Pippi Longstocking's Norwegian uncle. May I offer you some reindeer jerky while you're waiting?

Being a personal shopper is a dark art, with few tangible rewards. With the business spread by word of mouth, my clients would never admit they needed my assistance. Not even if they were put under torture. Let's be honest: who would admit to being in need of a style consultant?

People need advice, and, often a fresh point of view helps in rejuvenating a wardrobe that, with time, has become boring. But would they admit it? Not a chance!

It's like being an alcoholic: the first step is to admit you need help, and acknowledge that that pair of leggings, now you're in your mid-fifties, don't suit you any more. When you have recognised that, you're on the road to recovery, and my services will help you.

I started by chance, when I was in my late twenties. I'm a compulsive shopper, and I don't mean that in a derogatory way. The right to shop should be up there in the constitution (if I still lived in America, that is), just below the "free exercise of religion" and the "freedom of speech", and above the "right to keep and bear arms" (unless they come in different colours).

A sort of Amendment 1B: *Congress shall make no law in respect of the free exercise of shopping; or abridging the freedom of a shopping spree; or the right of the people peaceably to assemble (except during the sales period), and spend on clothes and shoes. Banks shall invest in the people's right to their pursuit of happiness, by means of fashion design.*

So the big question is, do I satisfy a potential customer – someone who might have thousands of pounds to spend – and forget my beliefs? Is it worth bending my ethics to please a client, just because we are in a post-recession period (and I actually need the money)?

The simple answer is, "NO. Never. Not a chance in hell. Zilch."

Dear Jasper,

Thank you for contacting me at GiGi-Personal Shopper. I reviewed your request for helping you to find a Norwegian jumper for this Christmas but, unfortunately, I have to decline the request.

As a Personal Shopper, I should inform you that we do not shop for specific items upon request. We prefer a more personal approach, where we spend time understanding our customer needs and have a full review of their current style in order to then propose suitable alternatives. It's a slow process, I suppose, that would not fit your requirements.

I appreciate the difficulties you might have encountered in finding the above-mentioned item. To be honest, I recollect my grandfather having one, a long time ago, but since then they seem to have entirely disappeared from the face of the earth.

I definitely have in my memory a scene from the Norwegian film "Troll i Ord", 1954, where they wear one. Since "The Eiger Sanction" (starring Clint Eastwood, 1975), where the main character moved on to wearing a neck jumper, fashion seems to have evolved, somewhat, inexplicably.

I asked my partner to research the matter, and I understand there are niche markets for the item you requested. Please see the attached list for websites and shops (mostly in Norway) that could fulfil your desire for tradition.

Warmest (if you find your jumper) regards

GiGi Griswald.

You might have wondered about my surname. My dad is Swedish with perhaps a sprinkle of German (hence the surname), while my mother is actually Italian. We also have a pinch of Maltese and French somewhere in our ancestry, but that's another story. I took my passion for clothes and fashion from my mother; otherwise, I would have had my own flat-pack clothes shop by now. What I found funny is that they called me Griselda, which means "Dark Battle" or some such in German. The reason behind that is still a mystery, and the two are not willing to give up the secret anytime soon.

I grew up in New York until I reached my tenth birthday, and then the family went back to Milan for a couple of years. The latter period was fundamental to my fashion imprinting, before we moved to the UK.

In my mid-twenties, I had what "they" call a credit-card problem. To me, it wasn't an issue at all, and although I admit I was late with my payments, I thought I was exercising my rights, as per Amendment 1B above. Unfortunately the Bank Manager, a little sad man with no sense of imagination or social compassion, thought otherwise. He gave me an ultimatum: repay your debts or else!!

At that time, I was working for a small firm of solicitors in Berkshire and I hated every minute of it. At school I wasn't great – not bad, but definitely not great. I found that many of the subjects were boring, or at least they were presented as such. No wonder I failed my GCSE in Domestic Economy – except I then become one of the most influential fashion trendsetters (not the dog) in the kingdom. Yeah, there is that little detail that I'm still not super-rich, but hey, the business is thriving, so no complaints there.

After a family meeting in my teens, we (?) decided that, owing to my non-bright school career, I should settle for a less demanding profession, and eventually the word "secretary" came out of someone's mouth; I don't remember whose. I was indeed fast at typing and quite smart, and during those years of teen-laziness, the job suited me well. Earning money was no longer an issue, except for the fact that I like shopping.

Yeah, you bet: by the tenth of the month I had made many shopkeepers happy. In some cases, I think I even contributed to sending some of their children to university, considering the amount of money I spent. Something needed to be done. In order to be successful in life, you need to have a plan. I had one, although maybe mine wasn't the smartest one.

My plan followed the dictate of the major business universities of the world, such as Harvard and Oxford, and was a "best of breed" in the industry. It was simple, clear and concise: I needed more money. As you can imagine, that didn't take me very far; after all, I was still a simple secretary. But even in the world of secretariat, people can progress and enhance. There are CEOs all over the country who need a bright mind to sort out their mess – what they call a Personal Assistant, which is nothing other than a secretary with a posh name and a hefty salary. You name it, the world was my oyster, and I only needed the right knife and right technique to open that damn mollusc. I needed to find my niche.

The first objective was really quite simple: find a job, get some experience under my Ferragamo pink belt, and then move on to a higher-paid job. After one year of window-shopping and struggle, I was ready to make my move. And so I did. The new job was paying a substantial three thousand pounds more a year (gross) than my first one. No more rummaging in the TK Maxx sale bargain bucket, like a homeless person in search of that discarded treasure in the bin, which never comes. No more scavenging the Primark department store in search of that shirt that, if well matched with a proper skirt and accessory, will not look cheap. Maybe I could even avoid delaying buying until the sale season. To be honest, I quite liked the word "season" associated with the sale one. That was a perfect description of me – a real bargain hunter, who lets the prey's population grow until it's time, and then goes in for the kill.

The reality hit me in the face two pay packets later, when I realised there was this guy going around called "Mr Inflation", who took all the fun out of my hard-earned, well-deserved salary. "Mr Inflation": a kryptonite who sucked all the spending power out of my wage.

The bastard.

A revised strategy was soon due, so I started working some evenings and weekends as a nanny. It wasn't going to earn much, or change my life, but, it gave a bit of oxygen to my finances, although I knew from the start that it would be more like the last breath on a sinking "Titanic" rather than a fresh breeze in the spring. But I landed distinctly well, with a Pakistani family not far from where I lived. At that point, I was still living with my parents in a decent-sized house near Bray. The neighbourhood was wealthy and in need of good, trustworthy nannies who could guard the precious and beloved children while their parents went out for a boozy night. They were family friends, lived across the road, and with a small push from Mum, there you go. I was hired.

******

If you want to continue reading Blue and Green Should Never Be Seen! (Or so Mother Says) you can find it at the same place that you purchased this book from. Happy reading!

If you want to keep up with the news of what is coming next please check my website at www.colettekebell.com to find out more.
You can also find my author pages at
https://www.goodreads.com/ColetteKebell
or
https://www.facebook.com/pages/Colette-Kebell/882613368417057
Or join me on twitter @colettekebell

I am still writing as I have enjoyed writing this as much as I hope you have enjoyed reading it. Thank you once again for buying my book and hopefully those that are to follow.

Lightning Source UK Ltd.
Milton Keynes UK
UKOW06f0325290815

257704UK00015B/190/P

9 780993 197130